THE MULTIVERSE *of Love*

THE MULTIVERSE *of Love*

K D PANDEY

Srishti
PUBLISHERS & DISTRIBUTORS

Srishti Publishers & Distributors
A unit of AJR Publishing LLP
212A, Peacock Lane
Shahpur Jat, New Delhi – 110 049

editorial@srishtipublishers.com

First published by
Srishti Publishers & Distributors in 2024

10 9 8 7 6 5 4 3 2 1

This is a work of fiction. The characters, places, organisations and events described in this book are either a work of the author's imagination or have been used fictitiously. Any resemblance to people, living or dead, places, events, communities or organisations is purely coincidental.

Printed and bound in India

If you want to find
the secrets of the universe,
think in terms of
energy, frequency, and vibration.

– Nikola Tesla

Chapter 1
The Dance of the Cosmos

Anika's Mundane Life

The sun's first rays hit the narrow streets of Mumbai, marking the beginning of another busy day. The air was thick with anticipation and the familiar scent of street food vendors preparing for the morning rush.

Enter Anika, a young woman in her mid-twenties with raven-black hair tied in a beautful messy bun, hurriedly getting ready for work. Anika has a unique sense of style that blends intelligence with practicality. She often styles her silky hair by pinning it up with a pencil, a simple yet clever touch that highlights her resourceful nature. Her glasses frame her face in a way that accentuates her sharp and knowledgeable appearance, making her look both smart and approachable. Anika's complexion is fair, and her soft pink lips add a gentle splash of color, enhancing her natural beauty. She prefers wearing hoodies, which lend her an easygoing and effortlessly cool vibe. Anika carries herself with a distinct confidence and moves through life with an elegant grace, making her stand out in any crowd. Her room, a reflection of her life, was *organized chaos* – books stacked in every possible corner, notes pinned on the walls, and half-drunk cups of tea forgotten on window sills.

Anika had a love-hate relationship with her alarm clock. This morning, it was especially antagonistic. “Five more minutes,” she groaned, pulling her blanket over her head. But the loud honks from the street below and the persistent calls of the local vegetable vendor ensured she had no choice but to start her day.

As she finally sat up, her cat, Chiku, took the opportunity to sneak under the blanket.

“Chiku! Not today! I have a Sanskrit class to teach!” she exclaimed, trying to untangle herself from the purring fur ball.

Her modest kitchen witnessed the most morning drama. Today, she burned her toast and spilled tea on her pink hooded T-shirt, and the blender decided to revolt by spewing a freshly made smoothie all over the counter. She sighed, “Ahh! Why can’t one morning be uneventful?”

On her way to the university, Anika’s auto-rickshaw broke down. “Just my luck,” she muttered. But Mumbai never lets one stay annoyed for long. An old man selling flowers on the corner saw her distress and handed her a marigold with a wink, “For good luck, madam.”

Her phone buzzed. It was a message from her mother:

Remember to visit the temple today. It’s your grandmother’s death anniversary.

Anika rolled her eyes; her mother’s reminders were never-ending. But beneath that exasperation was a warm affection. She quickly typed back.

I remember, Maa. And I promise no shoes inside this time!

She referred to a previous humorous temple mishap.

By the time Anika reached the university gates, she was running late. She burst into her classroom, expecting stern faces. Instead, her students stood with a birthday cake, singing. She laughed, “It’s not my birthday, you pranksters!”

A student, Rohan, grinned, "We know, ma'am. But after the week you've had, we believe you could use some cake."

The day continued in its comical, unpredictable fashion. There were surprise quizzes, unexpected rain showers, and even a pigeon making a nest in her office.

The world saw Anika as a Sanskrit scholar, a dedicated teacher, and a Mumbai resident navigating the city's quirky challenges. But beneath that exterior was a woman with dreams bigger than the city's skyline, a heart full of stories, and a soul itching to unravel the mysteries of the past. She often pondered, "There's got to be more to life than burnt toasts and mischievous cats." Little did she know, an adventure was just around the corner.

The Temple Revelation

The sun was just beginning to dip below the horizon as Anika made her way to the ancient temple of Shri Siddhivinayak. Nestled in the heart of Mumbai, this temple stood as a serene haven, bridging past traditions with the modern world. Its formidable stone walls, stained with time, were etched with stories that stretched back centuries.

Anika had always felt a deep connection to this place. Visits with her grandmother, tales of gods and goddesses, and the promise of a laddoo at the end had filled her childhood. Today, she was looking forward to a few moments of peace away from her chaotic life.

As she approached the temple, she was quickly engulfed in a whirlwind of activity. Devotees moved in a rhythmic flow, their voices merging into a soft hum of prayers and chants. The aroma of incense wafted through the air, mixed with the familiar smell of Mumbai's rains.

As she waited in line to offer her prayers, two elderly women ahead of her chatted animatedly. "I tell you, Rekha, kids these days and their mobile phones! My grandson, every minute, *tappa tappa* on that screen!"

Rekha chuckled, "You're telling me? My granddaughter tried to teach me WhatsApp. I told her I already have 'What's up?' every morning when I ask my knees!"

Anika suppressed her laughter, her worries momentarily forgotten.

Suddenly, a mischievous monkey leapt into the temple courtyard, its eyes darting around, assessing potential targets. The monkey made its way towards Anika. She watched with growing dread as it seemed to fixate on the garland she was holding. And in a swift motion, it snatched the garland and perched atop a pillar, examining its prize.

"Hey, little thief! That was for Vinayaka, not for you!" Anika exclaimed, hands on her hips.

A young boy nearby giggled. "Looks like Vinayaka sent his friend to collect his offering in person!"

The temple staff, adept at handling such shenanigans, began their strategic approach to retrieve the garland. But the monkey had other plans. With acrobatic flair, the monkey leapt off the pillar, dropping the garland and darting towards an 'old wooden chest'.

With the monkey finally appeased with some bananas and escorted away, Anika retrieved her garland. But something else caught her eye. Dislodged by the monkey's adventure, an old palm-leaf manuscript lay on the ground beside the wooden chest.

Intrigued, Anika picked it up, her fingers tracing the delicate inscriptions. The ancient Sanskrit script narrated a tale of cosmic connections and love transcending lifetimes. It mentioned two souls, Aditya and Lasya, whose love story was intertwined with profound wisdom.

"Ah, you've found the chronicles of Aditya and Lasya," said a voice from behind her.

She turned to see an elderly priest, his eyes reflecting eons of stories. "It's a tale few remember and even fewer understand. They journeyed together, not just in love but in seeking the profound secrets of our universe."

Anika's heart raced. "It's beautiful. I feel like it's calling out to me."

The priest smiled. "Sometimes, the universe has its playful ways of guiding us. Today, it chose a monkey. The manuscript is yours to study. Remember, it's not just about the words, but *the essence they capture*."

Overwhelmed, Anika whispered her thanks. As she stepped out after Vinayaka Darshan, the usual vastness of Mumbai's skyline stretched before her. Yet, she felt different, like she held a piece of the cosmos in her hands.

The monkey's antics, the laughter it induced, the temporary chaos, and finally, the serendipitous discovery of the manuscript – everything felt connected. And in that moment, Anika realized that life, with all its unpredictability, was a mosaic of moments and connections. And she was ready to embrace its rhythm.

The First Verses

Anika's apartment overlooked Mumbai's Marine Drive. The vast expanse of the Arabian Sea, with its rhythmic waves, always brought solace to her. But tonight, the sea, the twinkling lights of the city, and even the gentle breeze from her balcony weren't her primary concerns. Her focus was solely on the palm-leaf manuscript spread out on her living room floor.

She'd lit a few aromatic candles around to create the right ambience. "If I'm going to unravel ancient wisdom," Anika thought, "I might as well do it in style!"

The first verse was beautifully penned, but reading *ancient* Sanskrit was proving to be a task.

"Okay, let's break this down. *Ananta*... that means infinite. *Prem* is love. So, infinite love. Good start."

She continued translating, occasionally consulting a Sanskrit dictionary app on her phone. After about an hour, she had what she believed was a coherent English translation of the first verse.

> *'In the realm of infinite love, Aditya once asked for a mango from Lasya, and upon being offered the fruit, the skies danced with joy.'*

Anika blinked. "Seriously? This cosmic tale begins with... a mango? Maybe it's symbolic?" she pondered.

Anika called her friend Ravi, who had a doctorate in Ancient Indian Literature. "Ravi, I need your help. I'm translating this old manuscript, and something seems off."

Ravi, always up for a literary challenge, was intrigued. "Shoot."

She read out her translation. There was a pause, and then Ravi burst out laughing. "Anika, are you sure about this?"

"Hey, I tried my best! But a mango? Really? What's so cosmic about a mango?"

Ravi, still chuckling, replied, "Alright, let's break it down together. Come to Startbucks at Nariman Point."

Over the next hour, amidst a series of giggles, questionable translations, and some genuinely profound insights, the duo realized that Anika's initial interpretation had a few amusing errors.

"Aam in Sanskrit could mean 'mango,' but in this context, it meant 'common' or 'universal'," Ravi explained.

"So, it wasn't about a mango?" Anika face palmed, laughing.

"No, my dear fruit translator," Ravi teased. "*The verse speaks about a universal request from Aditya to Lasya, to which the universe responded with joy. It signifies their bond being in sync with cosmic harmony.*"

Anika sighed in relief. "Thanks, Ravi. I nearly turned a profound cosmic love story into a tale about fruit!"

Ravi left the café with a promise to help out at any time, but Anika continued to explore the manuscript.

The night was filled with more translations, some correct, others hilariously off-mark. But amidst all this, deep down, Anika realized something profound. The verses, while deep and insightful, were also filled with joy, love, and a touch of playfulness. It was as if the ancients knew that wisdom was best received with a light heart.

As she finally drifted off to sleep, the manuscript by her side, Anika felt a deep connection to Aditya and Lasya. Their story was unfolding, not just in the verses but in her own life, bringing humour, insights, and moments of profound clarity.

The dance of the cosmos, she realized, was not just in grand celestial events but also in everyday moments, shared laughter, and yes, even in misunderstood mangoes.

Enter Sharvil

It was a warm Saturday morning, and Anika's favourite café, 'Aromas of Mumbai', was bustling with the scent of fresh coffee, buttered toast, and the distant hum of local chatter created an ambience that Anika often found irresistible. As she poured over the manuscript, sipping her mocha coffee, she hardly noticed the figure that approached her table.

"Well, well, if it isn't Miss Mango Translator!" a familiar voice teased.

Anika looked up and rolled her eyes. A smile slowly spread across her lush, rosy lips. These lips, reminiscent of soft cherry blossoms, were perfectly shaped. Their plumpness was enhanced by a subtle gloss that made them gleam invitingly in the gentle light. "Sharvil! When did you get back from the States?"

Sharvil, with his sun-kissed tan, and Americanized accent but still very Indian at heart, was Anika's childhood friend. Having recently completed his post-graduation in Quantum Physics from MIT, Sharvil was the epitome of the modern, global Indian.

"Just last week. Yesterday, Ravi told me about the mangoes and now I can see you're still lost in your world of myths and legends." He signalled towards the manuscript.

Anika smirked. "It's not just any myths and legend; it's a deeply moving love story interwoven with cosmic wisdom."

Sharvil took a seat opposite her, a playful glint in his eyes. "So, enlighten me. What's so 'cosmic' about it?"

She began explaining the tale in excitement, the connection between Aditya and Lasya, and the deeper insights the verses held.

Sharvil leaned forward, "But don't you think, Anika, that all these ancient tales and scriptures are... well, outdated? We live in an age of science, technology, and evidence. Not stories."

Anika stirred her coffee, choosing her words. "Sharvil, just because something is ancient doesn't mean it lacks wisdom. These tales were perhaps our ancestors' way of understanding the universe, much like how Quantum Physics is yours."

Sharvil raised an eyebrow, intrigued. "So, you're comparing Quantum Physics with... mango tales?"

Anika laughed, "Not directly. But think about it. Quantum entanglement, for instance, talks about two particles being interconnected, no matter the distance. Isn't that similar to Aditya and Lasya's bond, two souls connected across realms?"

Sharvil considered this, "Interesting perspective. But *entanglement is proven. It's science. It's real.*"

Anika leaned in, "And who's to say the emotions, the experiences, the insights of our ancestors weren't real? Maybe science is just catching up!"

Their banter continued, shifting from playful taunts to deep discussions. Ancient views versus modern perspectives. For every logical argument Sharvil presented, Anika had a philosophical counter.

At one point, Sharvil, pretending to meditate, said, "Oh, wise one, enlighten this ignorant soul with your mango wisdom."

Anika, playing along, responded, "Young grasshopper, when you understand the mango, you'll understand the universe."

They both burst into laughter, drawing amused glances from neighbouring tables.

As the morning turned into afternoon, the essence of their conversation was clear: both ancient wisdom and modern science had their place.

Sharvil, with a sigh, finally said, "You know, Anika, it's good to be back. I missed our debates."

Anika smiled warmly, "Me too. And who knows, maybe through these debates, we'll find some answers. Or more questions. Either way, it'll be an adventure."

Sharvil nodded, "An adventure indeed. From mangoes to Quantum Physics."

They toasted their cups, celebrating not just their reunion but the joy of exploring the epic saga together.

A Glimpse into Aditya and Lasya

The next day, in her apartment, Anika decided, she'd dive deeper into the love story of Aditya and Lasya.

As Anika began to read, the ambience around her shifted subtly. The cacophony of the city faded, and the rhythmic pattern of raindrops transported her to a different realm – a pristine valley surrounded by majestic mountains, where time seemed to slow down.

Aditya, a calm and insightful young scholar, with deep-set eyes, found peace sitting by a lotus pond. Coming from a family of wise seers, he was deeply immersed in unravelling the mysteries of the universe and played the flute beautifully, reminiscent of a revered, flute-playing deity from ancient stories.

Lasya, the valley's beloved dancer, moved with such grace and beauty that she seemed to embody the universe's rhythm. Her eyes sparkled like stars, captivating everyone who watched her perform. Her dancing mirrored the eternal dance that keeps the universe in balance, enchanting all like the divine consort known from age-old legends. Together, Aditya's music and Lasya's dance brought a touch of the divine to their world.

One day, as Lasya danced by the pond, Aditya's meditation was gently interrupted by the soft tinkling of her anklets. He opened his eyes, and their gazes met. It wasn't just a casual meeting of two individuals, but a convergence of two souls. They felt an inexplicable connection, as if they were the two entangled particles Anika had mentioned to Sharvil.

Aditya smiled gently and said, "Your dance doesn't just move you, it feels like it's moving the whole universe... like creating and destroying the cosmos fabric at the same time."

Lasya, with a playful grin, responded, "And your music, wise scholar, seems to ripple through the universe, touching its very core."

One evening, as Aditya played his flute by the pond, the enchanting melodies drifted across the valley, weaving through the cool air. Lasya, returning from her dance practice, was drawn to the haunting beauty of the music. As she approached, their eyes met, sparking with recognition and excitement. A shared smile passed between them, and each felt a gentle tug at their heart—a profound connection that seemed to pull them closer. This moment marked the beginning of something special. Rooted in mutual admiration for each other's art and a shared reverence for the universe's beauty and mysteries, their serendipitous meeting ignited a bond that quickly deepened into love. Each found in the other a perfect companion for their creative and spiritual journeys.

Slowly, as days turned into nights and seasons ebbed and flowed, the bond between Aditya and Lasya deepened. They were inseparable, not in the sense of always being physically together, but in a way that they felt each other's presence even when apart. Their conversations spanned topics from the patterns of stars to the rhythm of heartbeats. It was as if, in their union, ancient wisdom met timeless love.

One evening, as they sat by the pond, with their foot in water, Lasya asked, "Aditya, do you think love, like ours, exists elsewhere in the universe?"

Aditya looked at the stars reflecting in the pond and softly said, "Lasya, our love is part of something bigger. Like the stars, we come together and share in life's dance. Our bond shows how deeply connected everything is."

Lasya leaned against Aditya, her head resting on his shoulder. "Then every moment we share, every little whisper, is a part of this great story of love."

As Anika read, she could almost feel the valley's cool breeze, hear the faint jingle of Lasya's anklets, and understand the depth of their conversations. She realized that the story wasn't just about Aditya and Lasya, but about anyone seeking connection, meaning, and love.

The rain had stopped, and the city sounds were coming back. But in Anika's heart, the story of Aditya and Lasya lingered, reminding her that love, in all its forms, endures beyond time and place.

The Missing Verse

Anika had been engrossed in the love story of Aditya and Lasya, cherishing every word, every emotion. But the next evening, as she flipped to the next page, she found a surprising emptiness. A page seemed to be missing. She recounted the pages, hoping it was just a misplaced one, but the realization soon set in. There was a gap in the story.

Anika thought back to the temple, the day she stumbled upon the manuscript. Was it complete when she found it? Did she miss a page during her hurried collection? Her thoughts raced.

She called Sharvil, hoping to bounce her frustration off him. The line trilled a few times before he picked up, "Anika? Everything okay?"

Anika sighed, "Sharvil, there's a missing page! I was reading about Aditya and Lasya's journey, and suddenly, there's a gap in the manuscript!"

Sharvil chuckled, "Well, dear Sherlock, maybe it's a test of your detective skills."

Anika, not in the mood for jokes, snapped, "It's not funny, Sharvil. The manuscript was in pristine condition, and now there's a missing page!"

Sharvil, sensing her distress, softened, "Okay, okay. Let's try to figure this out. Maybe revisit the temple?"

Anika nodded, "There's this elderly priest there; perhaps he might know something."

The next morning, under the warm Mumbai sun, Anika and Sharvil stood before the ancient temple. They approached the old priest, who was lighting incense sticks by the shrine.

Anika gently approached, "Namaste Babaji. I had found a manuscript here a few weeks ago. I believe there's a missing page."

The priest looked up, his eyes clouded with age but sharp with wisdom. "Ah, the story of Aditya and Lasya. It's said to be incomplete. Some say it's deliberate, others believe the last page was lost to time."

Anika's heart sank, "So there's no way to know the end?"

The priest smiled. "Who said anything about an end, child? Maybe it's a beginning."

Sharvil, trying to lift Anika's spirits, quipped, "So, maybe the missing page is like the director's cut? Only for special screenings?"

The priest, after thinking for a bit, spoke softly, "The story you found actually came from far away, from a small library in a village in Thrissur, Kerala. My ancestors brought it here a long time ago. If a page is missing, maybe it's still in that library or someone in the village has it. It looks like you might have to go there to find the rest of the story."

The priest spoke again, "My dear, sometimes it's the journey, the search, that's more important than the destination. If you want to know further, you may have to go to Kerala."

Anika looked at the manuscript in her hand, realizing that the story of Aditya and Lasya had not just been a tale to read, but an experience. It has also re-connected her with Sharvil, reignited her passion for ancient wisdom, and now presented a mystery.

With a grateful nod to the priest, she said, "Thank you, Babaji. Maybe the missing verse is a sign that every story has layers, waiting to be uncovered."

As Anika and Sharvil stepped out of the temple, Mumbai's rhythm embraced them. And even though a page was missing, the essence of the tale, its magic, lingered on, reminding them that stories, like life, were about the journey, not just the destination.

Sharvil's Reluctance

The next day, the aroma of freshly brewed coffee drifted through Anika's apartment. She and Sharvil sat on her balcony, sipping from their mugs, overlooking the busy Mumbai streets below. The manuscript lay between them, a silent testimony to the journey they'd already begun. Anika was bubbling with excitement, her eyes sparkling with the thrill of the chase.

"We should go to Kerala," she blurted out. "I've heard there are more manuscripts like this one there. Maybe we can find the continuation, the missing verse."

Sharvil nearly spat out his coffee. "Kerala?"

Anika rolled her eyes. "Come on, Sharvil! It's just a short flight. Plus, I've always wanted to see the backwaters and houseboats."

Sharvil leaned back, rubbing his temples dramatically. "Anika, I'm a Mumbai boy. I live by three main tenets: Traffic should be loud, the air should be thick with ambition, and water should only be in bottles or the sea."

She grinned, knowing he was half-joking. "Oh, come on! It'll be an adventure. You, me, and the ancient story of Aditya and Lasya. What's holding you back?"

Sharvil smirked, beginning his humorous list, "Well, for starters, the mosquitos in Kerala are the size of drones."

"And your point is?" Anika shot back.

"They might carry me away. You'd miss me," he deadpanned.

Anika snorted with laughter. "Alright, what's the next reason?"

"Coconuts," Sharvil stated gravely. "Dangerous things. They just... fall. I've heard stories."

"You'll wear a helmet," Anika retorted. "Anything else?"

Sharvil paused for effect, "Yes. The most important one. What if the spicy Kerala food is so delicious that I'll never enjoy our Mumbai street food again? It'll be a culinary catastrophe!"

She chuckled, "You're impossible! But if I promise to keep you safe from gigantic mosquitos, coconuts, and world-class spicy food, will you come with me?"

Sharvil sighed, feigning defeat. "Alright, but only if we can have coconut water by the backwaters."

Anika beamed, "That's the spirit! Kerala, here we come!"

They clinked their coffee mugs together, sealing the pact. The adventure was about to begin, and even with his comical reluctance, Sharvil was on board, proving that every journey, no matter the destination, is more enjoyable with a touch of humour and the right companion.

The Quantum Surprise

The quaint village library in Kerala was a world away from the busy life of Mumbai. Wooden shelves, teeming with age-old manuscripts and the intoxicating scent of parchment and ink, lined its walls. Anika and Sharvil had been directed there by a local historian, in hopes of finding any continuation or hint about their beloved story.

While Anika was engrossed in a manuscript, her fingers delicately flipping the pages, Sharvil was haphazardly browsing through another, his interest fading. That was until a certain verse caught his eye.

In the dance of love, their souls entwined,
Soulmates bound, in heart's sweet bind.
Across vast space, their spirits align,
A cosmic bond, forever defined...

The text hinted that Aditya and Lasya were deeply connected souls, not just by love, but by something even stronger—a bond that made their feelings and experiences reflect each other, no matter how far apart they were. It was as if they were from the same place, so when something happened to one, it instantly affected the other. Their hearts beat in sync like a modern idea of Quantum Physics, where two things are connected in a mysterious way, even when they're far apart.

Sharvil, ever the modern sceptic, couldn't help but smirk. "Hey Anika," he waved the manuscript. "Looks like our ancient poets were ahead of their time. This verse talks about two particles – or in this case, souls – being connected. Reminds me what you said about quantum entanglement."

Anika leaned over, her curiosity piqued. "Really? Let me see."

Reading aloud, she further began:

When seas vast part, their souls still dance,
Bound not just by heart, but by the universe's trance.
In the cosmic symphony, they find their stance,
Eternal bond, in love's sweet expanse.

Sharvil looked surprised, "That sounds a lot like the idea that two connected particles can instantly affect each other's states, no matter how far apart they are."

Quantum entanglement is like a magical connection between particles. Even if they're far apart, what happens to one instantly affects the other, almost like they're communicating faster than the speed of light. It's a strange and fascinating concept that still puzzles scientists today.

Anika's eyes were wide with wonder, "It's incredible to think ancient wisdom might've touched upon concepts we're only beginning to understand."

Sharvil, usually casual, was visibly excited now. "You know, if this is true, it might revolutionize the way we understand our ancient texts. They weren't just poetic, but perhaps scientific too, in their own metaphorical way."

A local librarian, who overheard them, came up with a smile, "Ah, the verses about connections in the universe. Many folks get curious about it. Some think it's just poetry, others believe it's ancient wisdom explaining the universe's secrets."

Anika, curious, asked, "Do you think ancient people knew about things like quantum mechanics?"

The librarian replied, "Maybe not exactly like how we see it now. But they had a sense of how everything in the universe is connected. They thought everything, even two people in love, is linked somehow."

Sharvil thought for a moment, "That's interesting. I thought these texts were just love stories, but now I'm seeing them differently, more scientifically. It's... humbling."

Anika then asked, "Excuse me, sir. I've been looking for clues about Aditya and Lasya's story, but it feels like we're still missing some important parts. Do you know where we could find the rest of the manuscript?"

Librarian: "Ah, young lady, the tale of Aditya and Lasya isn't easy to understand. It's spread out across the world like pieces of a puzzle. There was an old sage who tried to gather all these fragments, and that's how the manuscript was created. But before he could finish it, he was called away by someone named Kalanabha, and he left, leaving the manuscript incomplete."

"Who is Kalanabha?" she asked.

"I'm not sure. The sage didn't say much about him before he left," the librarian replied.

"So, you mean the complete story isn't in one place?" Anika was speechless.

"Exactly. You have to go on a journey, travelling to different places to gather clues. Every place you visit adds something new to the story, helping you understand Aditya and Lasya's love better."

"But where do I begin? How do I know where to look?"

The librarian sighed, "Fear not, my dear. The path ahead is clear. You must set forth to Varanasi, Jaipur, Hampi, and finally, to a monastery nestled in the majestic Himalayas. Each destination holds a key to unlocking a part of the story."

"Varanasi, Jaipur, Hampi, and the Himalayas... it sounds like quite the adventure."

"Indeed, Anika. But remember, it is through the journey itself that one truly comprehends the essence of the story. Embrace the unknown, and you shall discover the secrets that lie within."

As the day ended and the sun's golden light streamed through the library windows, Anika and Sharvil sat surrounded by ancient books, thinking about the wonders of the universe. What began as a search for a lost poem had now shown them how love, science, and the connections between things can open up endless possibilities.

Preparation for the Journey

Back in Mumbai, Anika, filled with excitement, immediately started planning the journey, poring over maps and making lists of essentials. She knew she couldn't on board on this adventure alone, and so she asked Sharvil to join her. Despite his initial reluctance, Sharvil couldn't bear the thought of leaving Anika to travel solo. Plus, the idea of spending more time with her was too appealing to pass up. And so, as Anika's apartment turned into a chaotic mess of travel gear and excitement.

"Sharvil, have you seen my sun hat?" Anika's voice floated from her bedroom, half-muffled by the piles of clothes surrounding her.

From the living room, engrossed in a travel blog on his tablet, Sharvil responded, "Why do you need a sun hat? We're not going to the Sahara!"

Anika emerged, holding up the wide-brimmed hat, "It's stylish! Plus, protection from the sun."

Sharvil chuckled, "Two birds, one stone, huh?"

A knock on the door interrupted their banter, signalling the arrival of yet another package. Anika hurried to receive it, returning with a large box. "Ah! The hand-held GPS and NavIC I ordered. Sharvil, I told you, I've got you covered."

Sharvil eyed the box sceptically. "Do we really need both?"

She winked, "Just being prepared!"

Their packing was interspersed with light bickering and lots of laughter. Anika would insist on packing three types of sunscreens, while Sharvil would try to sneak in his favourite snacks, arguing that he might not survive without Mumbai's spicy treats.

"That can be arranged," Anika smiled, scribbling it down. "But no deviations for street food tasting!"

Sharvil feigned shock, "You wound me, Anika! Food is an essential part of any journey."

Their cheerful talk went on as they figured out their route, where to go, and where to stay. But beyond the fun of packing, they were bubbling with excitement. They weren't just searching for a lost manuscript; they were also stumbling into the realms of love, science, and ancient stories, without even meaning to.

As the evening turned to night, Anika paused, looking around her apartment turned war zone. "You know, amidst all this chaos, I feel... happy. I haven't felt this alive in years."

Sharvil, pausing in his attempt to fit his shoes into his already overflowing bag, looked up. "Me too. There's something about this journey, Anika. It's not just about the manuscript anymore. It's about rediscovery, understanding, and maybe... just maybe, finding a piece of ourselves we didn't know was missing."

She smiled, touched by his words, "Well, then. Here's to finding missing verses and missing pieces."

He raised his coffee mug in agreement, "And to sunscreens and sun hats."

Anika hesitated, "Sharvil... I was thinking... what do you say we take the train this time instead of flying?"

Sharvil thought about it for a moment and said, "Hmm, train? But isn't flying faster and more convenient?"

Anika nodded but with a wistful look on her face said, "True, but there's something about train travel, you know? It's slower, yes, but it allows us to really soak in the journey. We'll get to watch the world go by, see different landscapes, and maybe even meet some interesting people along the way."

Sharvil smiled, "That does sound nice. And it could give us more time to just... be together."

Anika blushed slightly, "Yeah, exactly! Just you and me, sharing moments and making memories as we travel."

Sharvil felt warm in his heart, "I like the sound of that. Plus, it'll be an adventure in itself, "Yeah, I'm in. And who knows, maybe we'll discover something new about ourselves along the way."

They laughed, their companionship clearly visible. encapsulating the spirit of adventure, friendship, and the joy of the unexpected.

Setting Off

The next morning was fresh, and Mumbai's famous hustle was already alive. Street vendors were setting up, morning walkers strolled past, and the unmistakable aroma of freshly brewed tea wafted through the air. But amidst this routine, there was a palpable sense of excitement outside Anika's apartment.

Sharvil, donning a pair of sunglasses, stood next to an auto-rickshaw, holding onto two large bags, one of which seemed to have a few snacks peeping out. "Anika, come on! At this rate, we'll start our journey next year!"

From the doorway, Anika emerged, clutching her bag, adjusting the sun hat, and looking every bit the travel enthusiast. "Oh, hush! Good things take time."

He snickered, "Like you choosing between two almost identical pairs of shoes?"

She smirked, “Precisely! A girl needs options.”

Handing a bag to the auto driver, Anika continued, “By the way, I got our train tickets.”

Sharvil raised an eyebrow, “Train? Anika, my modern city girl, wants to travel by train.”

She giggled. “For the experience! And, again think about it: the rhythm of the tracks, picturesque landscapes, and local food at every station... it’ll be beautiful.”

They climbed into the auto, and as it began to move, the noise of the city slowly merged into a harmonious background. The streets of Mumbai, always alive with activity, seemed to be wishing them well on their adventure.

In the Kashi Express train, they found their AC First Class berths opposite each other. Anika, ever the planner, immediately started organising her little space, setting out a book and a water bottle, while Sharvil was more interested in the food vendors passing by.

“Look at this!” He held up a spicy vada pav. “The best thing about trains? The food!”

She rolled her eyes but couldn’t resist a smile. “You and your stomach!”

As the train started to move, the rhythm of the wheels seemed to sync with the beats of their excited hearts. The journey had begun.

The landscape outside was mesmerising. Lush fields, kids waving as they passed and rivers reflecting the golden hue of the sun. They spent hours just looking out, occasionally pointing out interesting sights to each other.

During one such moment, Anika turned thoughtful. “You know, Sharvil, this journey, it’s like life. We’re always moving. But we don’t always appreciate the beauty along the way.”

Sharvil, munching on a snack, looked at her, "Deep thoughts over the Indian countryside?"

She nudged him, "I'm serious! Think about it."

He nodded, "You have a point. And maybe, that's what Aditya and Lasya's story is about. Not just the culmination of their love, but the journey they took together, the universe they explored?"

Anika beamed, "Exactly! It's not just about the end but the moments that lead to it."

They spent the evening sharing stories, laughing over childhood memories, and discussing the verses they'd come across. As night fell and the compartment lights dimmed, the soft glow seemed to envelop them in a cocoon of warmth.

Outside, the world raced by, but inside, time seemed to stand still. For Anika and Sharvil, the journey had become more than just finding a missing verse; it was a shared exploration of life love, and the mysteries of the universe.

As they drifted off to sleep to the lullaby of the moving train, there was a sense of hopeful anticipation. The next day held the promise of new discoveries, and together, they were ready to embrace whatever came their way.

Chapter 2
Exploration

Varanasi Vignettes

The train wheeled into Varanasi, its ancient echoes felt even in the busy clamour of the station. Anika and Sharvil alighted with wide-eyed wonder, their bags slung over their shoulders.

Sharvil took a deep breath, "You can really feel the history here."

Anika grinned, "You mean the smell of chola samosas and malaiyo?"

"No, beyond that," he chuckled. "The air feels dense with stories."

As they made their way through the crowded streets, the duo was captivated by the symphony of sounds – temple bells ringing, vendors calling out their wares, children laughing.

Sharvil, always one to go with the flow, suddenly paused. "Look, Anika! A barbershop! Maybe I should get a shave?"

She raised an eyebrow, "You? A shave? Here?"

"Why not?" he grinned, and before she could react, he'd plopped himself down in the old, rickety barber's chair under a Peepal tree.

The elderly barber, with a twinkle in his eyes, began prepping him. He noticed Anika's apprehensive look and laughed,

"Don't worry, madam. I've been shaving faces longer than he's been alive."

As the barber skilfully worked, a group of children gathered around, intrigued by the scene. One of them whispered to Anika, "He looks like a hero from the movies now!" Anika chuckled, taking a sneaky photo.

Sharvil's face was fresh and tingling. They paid the barber and continued their walk. Suddenly, a feisty old woman caught Anika's attention. She was selling flower garlands for temple offerings.

"Come, dear," she beckoned. "Buy a garland. It will bring you good luck."

Anika hesitated but Sharvil nudged her, "Go on! Maybe it'll help in our search."

As Anika picked out a garland, the old woman leaned in closer, "You know, dear, these flowers have seen many lovers unite. Just like you two." She winked.

Sharvil blushed, "Oh no—"

Anika cut him off, "Thanks for the garland!"

As Anika and Sharvil made their way through the vibrant streets of Varanasi, they found themselves wandering through the narrow lanes of Godowlia Market. The narrow streets were teeming with activity, lined with an array of shops and stalls selling everything from colourful silk fabrics to intricately carved wooden souvenirs.

Anika's eyes sparkled with curiosity as she saw the offerings of the local vendors. She couldn't resist stopping at the famous Shyam Sundar Sari Emporium, known for its exquisite silk sarees adorned with intricate zari work. Nearby, Sharvil also found himself drawn to the enchanting melodies drifting from the music shop, where traditional instruments like the tabla and sitar were on display.

The aroma of street food was filling the air, tempting Anika and Sharvil to try the local delicacies. They indulged in piping hot kachoris from Ram Bhandar, a popular eatery tucked away in one of the market's narrow alleys, and savoured the sweet flavours of the famous malaiyo, a traditional dessert made from milk and saffron.

As they roamed through the maze-like lanes of Godowlia Market, Anika and Sharvil couldn't help but marvel at the vibrant mosaic of sights, sounds, and smells that surrounded them. Each corner revealed some new treasures to explore, from intricate beadwork at the Shri Krishna Beads & Bangles shop to fragrant incense sticks at the Divine Fragrances store.

With every step, they discovered new facets of the city's vibrant personality, leaving them eager to continue their exploration of this enchanting destination.

After their exploration of Godowlia Market, Anika and Sharvil made their way to the famous Kashi Vishwanath Temple, one of the holiest sites in Varanasi. The temple, dedicated to Lord Shiva, stood tall amidst the busy streets, its towering spire reaching towards the heavens.

As they entered the sacred precincts of the temple, Anika and Sharvil found themselves surrounded by an aura of spirituality and reverence. The air was filled with the sound of bells chiming and devotees offering prayers, creating an atmosphere of devotion and tranquillity.

Anika marvelled at the intricate architecture of the temple, with its ornate carvings and exquisite sculptures depicting scenes from Hindu mythology. Sharvil was captivated by the sanctity of the surroundings, feeling a sense of peace wash over him as he soaked in the divine energy of the temple.

As they explored, they came across the revered figure of Kashi Kotwal, the guardian deity of Varanasi. An ancient legend spoke of Kashi Kotwal's unwavering vigilance in safeguarding the city from evil forces, his divine presence serving as a symbol of protection and spiritual strength for the residents of Varanasi.

Anika and Sharvil offered their prayers to Lord Shiva and Kashi Kotwal, seeking blessings for their journey ahead. As they bowed their heads in reverence, they felt a deep sense of gratitude for the opportunity to experience the spiritual richness of Varanasi and the timeless devotion of its people.

The next stop was the famous Dashashwamedh Ghat. The serene sight of the Ganges, with devotees taking a dip, and priests performing rituals, was truly captivating. Anika and Sharvil decided to go on a boat ride.

Their boatman, Ramesh, was a jolly fellow, "You two on honeymoon?"

Sharvil coughed, "No, just friends!"

Ramesh winked, "That's what they all say."

The boat gently glided on the river, and Anika lost in thought, whispered, "It's so peaceful here."

Sharvil smiled, "Yes, amidst all the chaos, there's a strange tranquillity."

As the boat gently floated on the calm Ganga River, Anika and Sharvil felt a peacefulness wash over them. They listened to the gentle sounds of the water and distant temple bells and watched as the sunset painted the sky with beautiful colours. In that quiet moment, surrounded by the ancient city of Varanasi, they felt completely at ease, as if the river itself was telling them stories of peace and happiness.

After the boat ride, they went to a tea stall. The tea vendor regaled them with tales of famous personalities he'd supposedly served, "*Amitabh jab aaye the to yahi chai piye the.*"

By evening, as they sat on the ghats, watching the famous Ganga Aarti, Anika sighed, "Varanasi is magical, isn't it?"

Sharvil nodded, "Every corner has a story. Every face, a tale."

Their day had been a mix of laughter, sightings, and cultural revelations. Varanasi, with its quirks and charms, had left an indelible mark on their hearts. As they headed back to their Hotel, the city's vibrant background continued to unfold around them, promising more adventures in the days to come.

Spiritual Surprises

After their delightful escapades on their first day in Varanasi, at night, Anika thought it might be a good idea to engage in something a bit more spiritual. She went to her room, "Sharvil, we're in the spiritual capital of India. How about we try a meditation class tomorrow morning?"

Sharvil choked on his water, "Meditation? Do you seriously think I can sit still for more than two minutes?"

Anika giggled, "Well, we won't know unless we try, right?"

"Okay. I am in," said Sharvil.

The next day, early in the morning, both found themselves in a quaint Mandakini ashram by the river, seated in a circle, surrounded by people of different ages and nationalities. The meditation guru, a serene man named Acharya Vimal, entered the room and greeted everyone with a soft 'Namaste'.

Sharvil leaned over to Anika and whispered, "Do you think he's going to make us levitate or something?"

Anika elbowed him gently, "Shush, and keep an open mind!"

Acharya Vimal began the session by explaining the essence of meditation:

> "Pay attention to your thoughts. Don't try to control them or repeat any words or names. Just observe whatever your mind is doing. Let it be, don't interfere or push it away; just observe. You just need to be a silent observer, and this act of observing is meditation.

"As you observe, you'll notice your mind gradually becoming less cluttered with thoughts. But you won't fall asleep; instead, you'll become more awake and aware.

"When your mind is completely empty, you'll feel a surge of energy and awareness. This heightened awareness is the result of meditation. So you could say meditation is simply observing, without judging or analysing. Just by observing, you'll find yourself stepping out of the realm of the mind."

Sharvil's eyes started wandering, admiring the paintings on the walls and the birds outside the window.

"Close your eyes," the Acharya's calm voice instructed.

While Anika easily sank into a deep state of relaxation, Sharvil was having a field day inside his head. Did I lock the room? What's for breakfast? Oh, I should've worn the other shirt.

About twenty minutes in, a loud snore echoed in the silent room. Eyes fluttered open and suppressed giggles filled the room. Anika peeked through her lashes to see Sharvil, head tilted back, mouth wide open, snoring away. Acharya Vimal, with a twinkle in his eye, simply said, "Some find peace quicker than others." Everyone burst into laughing.

After the session, as they walked out, Anika couldn't help but tease, "Reached nirvana, did we?"

Sharvil blushed, "Hey, at least I was peaceful."

Later that day, Anika had another idea. "Why don't we join a yoga class in the afternoon? It's meant to be refreshing!"

Sharvil sighed, "After our 'peaceful' morning? No thanks. I'll just head back to the hotel and relax."

Anika didn't want to go back to the hotel, but she also didn't want to push Sharvil. After all, he had come along for her sake.

Clue Conundrum

The next morning sunlight danced on the rippling waters of the Ganges as Anika and Sharvil savoured the flavours of masala chai and freshly made kachoris in a quaint café overlooking the river. The spiritual aura of Varanasi seeped into their souls, stirring a thoughtful mood in Sharvil.

Anika, noticing the pensive expression on Sharvil's face, gently asked, "You seem lost in thought. What's on your mind?"

Sharvil took a sip of his chai before responding, "It's just... the energy of this city, it's different, isn't it? It feels like there's more to discover beyond the surface."

Anika nodded, understanding his sentiments. "Varanasi has a way of revealing its mysteries to those who seek them. Shall we explore further?" Sharvil didn't want to say no to Anika again, so, he agreed to it.

After their leisurely breakfast, they decided to explore further and stumbled upon the Shri Kashi Karvat Temple. Unlike other temples in Varanasi, this one didn't resonate with the usual sounds of prayers or the ringing of bells. It stood quietly on the Dattatreya Ghat near Manikarnika Ghat, its presence mysterious and intriguing.

As they approached the temple, they noticed its unique charm. Situated near the river, it seemed to have a life of its own. The Ganga's water level sometimes rose, causing the temple to dip underwater, creating a magical sight. Yet, despite its enchanting allure, no one seemed to worship here. Legends spoke of curses, making it impossible for prayers to be offered.

Standing for 300 years, the temple had a surprising tilt to its structure, reminiscent of the Leaning Tower of Pisa. Despite facing floods and gathering soil, it remained resilient, earning the affectionate nickname 'Kashi Karvat' from the locals.

Intrigued by its history, Anika and Sharvil ventured towards it. As they approached the temple, Anika remarked, "There's something intriguing about this place, don't you think?"

Sharvil glanced at the temple's unique tilt and nodded in agreement. "Definitely. It's as if it holds secrets from centuries past."

As they stepped into the temple, Anika and Sharvil felt an aura of ancient wisdom surrounding them. The priest, sensing their curiosity, greeted them warmly. Anika, her eyes gleaming with anticipation, asked the priest about the legendary love story of Aditya and Lasya.

The priest smiled kindly, "I don't have much knowledge about their story, but I do possess a few ancient manuscripts that might shed some light on the matter. They contain age-old rituals and customs that have been passed down through generations."

Sharvil's interest piqued, and he eagerly inquired, "Could these manuscripts hold clues about the bond between Aditya and Lasya?"

The priest nodded thoughtfully, "It's possible. These rituals and customs often reflect the values and beliefs of the time they originated from. Perhaps they might offer insights into the timeless love that transcends generations."

Anika, feeling a surge of excitement, exclaimed, "Let's examine these manuscripts! Who knows what secrets they might reveal about Aditya and Lasya's enduring love?"

With a sense of anticipation, they followed the priest to where the ancient manuscripts were kept, ready for a discovery that would unravel the mysteries of the past and illuminate the path to understanding the eternal bond of Aditya and Lasya. The priest handed over a few scripts to them.

They sat on Dattatreya Ghat, Anika pulled out the manuscript, her fingers caressing its fragile leaves.

In the rhythm's sway, where dancers twirl,
A quantum dance, in cosmic play,
Entangled steps, in the quantum array.
In every leap, a universe spins,
Infinite possibilities, where love begins.
In the dance of souls, entwined in grace,
Quantum echoes, in timeless space.

Anika's eyes widened with wonder as she made a connection, "It's fascinating how these rituals reflect the harmony and balance of the universe, just like Aditya's music and Lasya's dance."

Sharvil, ever the curious thinker, chimed in, "It's almost like they were tapping into some kind of cosmic energy, something beyond our understanding. Indeed, these rituals were thought to align with the natural rhythms of the universe, much like the principles of quantum science that we explore today."

Anika's mind buzzed with excitement, "So, you mean these ancient rituals could somehow be linked to modern quantum concepts? Like how particles are entangled across vast distances?"

Sharvil smiled, "Maybe... Just as particles can influence each other instantaneously, these rituals may represent a deeper connection between souls that transcends time and space."

Anika nodded thoughtfully, "So, Aditya and Lasya's love wasn't just a romantic tale but something much larger, something that resonates with the very fabric of the universe."

Anika rolled her eyes playfully. "We need to figure out our next destination. Look here," she pointed at a passage in the manuscript. It read:

When the river meets the setting sun,
To the land of the desert, you must run.
Where water is more precious than gold,
Seek the tale that's yet to be told.

This manuscript isn't a mere love story; it's also a treasure map of sorts."

Sharvil smirked, "From zen master to Indiana Jones, quite the transition!"

Sharvil read aloud, attempting a dramatic tone, "Sounds like we're heading to a desert. Rajasthan, perhaps?"

Anika contemplated, "It does seem likely. But there's more. This part intrigues me." She pointed to another passage:

In the city of victory, find your way,
To the tower of silence, before the break of day.
Whispered secrets of a time long gone,
Will show the path you need to be on.

"City of victory... tower of silence," Sharvil mused. "Jaipur is known as the 'Victory City', isn't it? And the 'tower of silence'... could it be a literal tower?"

Anika pursed her lips in thought. "Or it could be metaphorical. A place of quiet reflection amidst the mayhem, maybe."

Sharvil's face lit up. "The Birla Mandir! It's in Jaipur, and I've heard it's a serene place, amidst all the hustle and bustle."

They both shared an excited glance, realizing they might be on the brink of something monumental. Anika carefully tucked the manuscript away, her heart racing with anticipation.

Their playful banter resumed as they began planning. "You know, you might just be the brains of this operation," Anika teased.

Sharvil feigned a pout, "Oh, so I wasn't before?"

Anika chuckled, "You were the... charm."

A soft blush coloured Sharvil's cheeks. "Well, in that case, let's charm our way to Jaipur!"

"Let's uncover history's best-kept secret."

The journey had slowly been taking a more profound meaning for them. Now, it wasn't just about the manuscript anymore. It was about two souls, united by fate, attempting to unravel an age-old mystery.

And so, with cryptic verses as their guide and an ancient city behind them, they set their sights on the sandy horizons of Rajasthan, eager to dig deeper to understand the tale of Aditya and Lasya.

Jaipur Revelations

Anika and Sharvil found themselves seated in the elegant ambience of Suvarna Mahal, Jaipur, the luxurious setting a stark contrast to their casual attire. As they enjoyed their afternoon tea, the manager approached their table, drawn by the air of intrigue surrounding the couple.

"Good afternoon, esteemed guests," the manager greeted with a warm smile. "What brings you to our humble abode today?"

Anika, impressed by the hotel's grandeur, replied, "We're exploring Jaipur and its rich history. But we're also on a quest for something more... ancient and mysterious."

The manager's eyes sparkled with interest. "Ah, in that case, might I suggest venturing beyond Jaipur's well-trodden paths? There lies a place of profound significance, shrouded in mystery and ancient wisdom."

Sharvil leaned in, intrigued by the manager's cryptic words. "Where might that be?"

The manager's smile widened, "*To the tower of silence*," he said, his tone tinged with reverence. "Or as some might call it, the Dilwara Jain Temple."

Anika and Sharvil exchanged a curious glance. So the '*tower of silence*' meant Dilwara Jain Temple. Their interest was piqued by the enigmatic suggestion. With a nod of gratitude to the manager, they made the spontaneous decision to heed his advice and explore the mystical allure of Dilwara Jain Temple, hopeful that it would offer the answers they sought in their quest for ancient wisdom and hidden truths.

The air was thick with anticipation as they approached the magnificent structure, its marble facade glowing in the fading light. Stepping into the temple complex, they were immediately struck by the intricate carvings adorning every surface. Each pillar, every archway, seemed to tell a story of ancient wisdom and divine beauty. Anika couldn't help but marvel at the craftsmanship, tracing her fingers along the delicate patterns etched into the marble.

Sharvil, ever the sceptic turned enthusiast, was equally captivated. "These carvings are extraordinary," he remarked, his voice filled with wonder. "It's as if each stone holds a piece of history, waiting to be discovered."

Their guide, a knowledgeable Jain scholar, led them through the temple, explaining the significance of the carvings and the principles of Jain philosophy. Anika listened intently, absorbing every word, while Sharvil asked insightful questions, eager to understand more.

Sharvil pointed to the temple ceiling, exclaiming, "Doesn't it resemble the Arc reactor from Marvel movies?" Anika glanced up, considering his observation. "Perhaps," she replied, "but our focus should be on something connected to Aditya and Lasya."

As they wandered through the temple halls, surrounded by the serene atmosphere of devotion, Anika felt a sense of peace wash over her. It was as if the ancient wisdom of the carvings was speaking to her soul, guiding her towards a deeper understanding of herself and the world around her.

At one point, they came across a particularly intricate carving depicting the cycle of birth and rebirth, a central tenet of Jain belief. Anika found herself drawn to it, feeling a strange sense of recognition as she gazed upon the ancient symbols.

"It's like Aditya and Lasya's story," she mused, turning to Sharvil. "A continuous cycle of love, loss, and renewal, spanning across lifetimes."

Sharvil nodded in agreement, his eyes alight with understanding. "Just like the carvings here, their story is engraved into the multiple dimensions of the universe, or the multiverse, waiting to be discovered by those who seek it."

Anika began, her voice was soft and contemplative. "It's so timeless. I mean, living in different timelines yet feeling so connected."

Sharvil nodded, "It's profound. To think that love could transcend time and space. But, what's more intriguing is how their love story seems to parallel the principles of quantum entanglement."

Anika looked puzzled. "Quantum what now?"

Sharvil chuckled. "Quantum entanglement. It's a phenomenon where particles become interconnected. The state of one particle is dependent on the state of the other, no matter the distance between them, even if they are beyond the limit of one galaxy. Their connection is instantaneous."

Anika's eyes widened in realization. "That sounds a lot like Aditya and Lasya's connection! They're entangled souls."

After a pause, Sharvil said, "You know, Anika, we've known each other for a while now. Have you ever felt... entangled?"

She turned to face him, her face lit up by the glow of the setting sun. "What do you mean?"

Sharvil hesitated, twirling a piece of the manuscript between his fingers. "I mean, our paths crossing, this journey, this story – it feels like more than mere coincidence."

Anika looked down hiding her blushing face, her fingers tracing patterns on the wall. "I've always believed in serendipity, Sharvil. Maybe this is our version of it."

He took a deep breath, the weight of his next words heavy on his chest. "I've always felt a pull towards you, Anika. Since the day we met. Like something in us recognized each other. It sounds so cliché, but I feel... somewhat connected."

She met his gaze, her eyes searching his. "Sharvil..."

He quickly interrupted, "I know, I know. We're on this quest, and it's not the best time. But being in this city, between all its spiritual energy, I felt compelled to confess."

Anika finally whispered, "Sharvil, I won't lie. I've felt it too. A connection. A pull. But I've been afraid."

He reached out, placing a hand over hers. "Afraid of what?"

She sighed. "Of losing what we have. Of complicating things. So I always relied on being your BFF."

Sharvil's thumb caressed her hand. "Life's too short for what-ifs, Anika. If our quest has taught us anything, it's to seize the moment."

Anika chuckled, "That's deep, coming from Mr Sceptic."

He grinned. "Guess this place is changing me."

As they journeyed away from Dilwara Temple, Anika felt a sense of determination settle over her. Glancing at the passing landscape, she turned to Sharvil, who seemed lost in thought.

"Hey, Sharvil," she began, breaking the silence. "While we're on the road, I thought it might be wise to plan our next destinations. We wouldn't want to miss out on anything significant like we did in Jaipur."

Sharvil nodded, snapping out of his reverie. "Good idea. Where do you think we should go next?"

Anika took out her notebook and started looking through it. She said, "'I did some searching and found two places. First, there's Hosur and Mysuru. People there are really good at making beautiful jewellery and trinkets. Also, they have lots of art and music. I thought we could check out their stuff, maybe find something that reminds us of Aditya and Lasya's love story."

Sharvil seemed interested. He asked, "That sounds cool, and what about those hidden chambers in the Mysuru Palace?"

Anika smiled, glad that Sharvil was engaged in the planning process. "Exactly! I read about these secret chambers rumoured to hold love letters and poems penned by lovelorn souls, echoing the sentiments expressed by Aditya and Lasya."

With their next destinations mapped out and a renewed sense of purpose, Anika and Sharvil continued their journey, eager to uncover more mysteries and dive deeper into the timeless love story that seemed to transcend time.

Hampi Hurdles

As Anika and Sharvil stood before the majestic Virupaksha Temple in Hampi, part of the Group of Monuments at Hampi, designated as a UNESCO World Heritage Site, they marvelled at its grandeur. Sharvil eagerly shared some fascinating insights he had discovered about the temple's unique musical pillars.

"Anika, did you know that these musical pillars are not just ordinary stone columns? They're marvels of ancient engineering! Each pillar is intricately carved with elaborate patterns and designs, but that's not all. When you tap them, they produce a variety of musical tones, almost like a musical instrument!"

Anika's eyes sparkled with curiosity. "That's incredible, Sharvil! How do they work?"

Sharvil explained, "Well, these pillars are made of different types of stone, each with its own density and composition. When you strike them with your hand or a small wooden stick, they vibrate at specific natural frequencies, producing distinct musical notes. It's like they're tuned to create harmony!"

Anika nodded in amazement. "So, it's not just about the carvings; it's about the materials used too. No wonder they sound so magical!"

"Exactly!" Sharvil exclaimed. "And here's the really mind-blowing part: each pillar produces a different sound, ranging from deep, resonant tones to high-pitched melodies. Some say it's like playing a giant xylophone!"

Anika grinned, imagining the enchanting sounds reverberating through the temple. "I can almost hear the music now, Sharvil. It must be a surreal experience to stand amidst all that ancient melody."

Sharvil nodded enthusiastically. "Exactly, Anika! It's like being transported back in time, surrounded by centuries-old tunes. It's no wonder these pillars have fascinated people from across the world for generations."

As Anika and Sharvil walked near the serene water body outside the Virupaksha Temple in Hampi, Sharvil couldn't contain his excitement. "Anika, did you know that the Virupaksha Temple is not just famous for its musical pillars, but it also showcases a remarkable scientific phenomenon?"

Anika's curiosity was piqued. "Really? What is it?"

Sharvil began to explain, his voice filled with enthusiasm. "It's called the Pinhole Camera Effect. You see, the shadow of the temple's tower falls inverted inside the opposite wall of the temple through a lens-like hole structure. It's like a natural camera obscure!"

Anika's eyes widened with wonder. "That's incredible! How does it work?"

"Let me break it down for you," Sharvil said, eager to boast off his knowledge. "When light falls on the temple tower, it creates a shadow. But instead of forming in front of the tower, the shadow passes through a small opening on the wall, acting like a mirror or a lens. This causes the image to appear inverted on the opposite wall."

Anika nodded, trying to visualize the concept. "So, it's like the temple itself is a giant camera?"

"Exactly!" Sharvil exclaimed. "And what's even more fascinating is that the shadow cast has a pinch of golden colour, adding to the mystique of the phenomenon. It's like a testament to the ingenuity of our ancestors."

Anika marvelled at the ingenuity of ancient architecture. "It's amazing how they could incorporate scientific principles into their designs."

Sharvil nodded in agreement. "Absolutely. And speaking of design, did you know that the temple also showcases mathematical concepts like fractals?"

Anika's interest was piqued. "Fractals? What are those?"

"Fractals are patterns that repeat themselves at different scales," Sharvil explained. "And the main shape of the temple is triangular, but as you look up, the patterns divide and repeat themselves, much like a snowflake."

Anika looked up at the intricate patterns adorning the temple's facade, marvelling at the mathematical precision. "It's incredible how they were able to incorporate such complex concepts into their architecture."

Sharvil smiled, feeling a deep sense of connection to the temple and its rich heritage. "Indeed. The Virupaksha Temple is not just a place of worship; it's a living testament to the brilliance of ancient Indian civilisation."

As they sat by the water body, surrounded by the sounds of ancient melodies and the awe-inspiring beauty of the temple,

Anika and Sharvil felt a profound connection to the rich cultural heritage of India. At that moment, they realized that music and science were not just separate disciplines but intertwined aspects of a shared human experience, transcending time and space.

Ancient Scripts and Misfits

Leaving behind the laughter of Hampi for the solemn silence of history, Anika and Sharvil arrived at the next destination, the tranquil town of Mysuru. Known for its palaces, it also boasted ancient libraries housing some of India's most valued manuscripts.

In the grand halls of the Mysuru Palace, Anika and Sharvil started their quest for ancient treasures,

As they wandered through the palace's corridors, adorned with ornate paintings and steeped in the weight of centuries past, they felt a sense of reverence for the secrets waiting to be uncovered.

Sharvil, adjusting his sunglasses, remarked, "So, the library, again?

Anika grinned, "No. But imagine what treasures those manuscripts might hide, if it is there!"

An elderly caretaker, Mr Sharma, greeted them warmly, his eyes gleaming with curiosity as Anika explained their mission. "Ancient love tales, you say?" he mused. "Follow me, I'll show you something that might pique your interest, a section with manuscripts that are over a millennia old. Perhaps one may belong to something which you are looking for."

In a hidden chamber deep within the palace, they discovered a trove of love letters and poems, carefully preserved by time. Anika's heart raced with excitement as she examined each delicate page, her fingers tracing the faded ink of lovelorn souls.

But it was the symbols adorning the pages that caught her eye – an anklet and a blue stone, etched with meaning and mystery.

"Sharvil, look!" she exclaimed, her voice barely above a whisper. "These symbols... they're just like the ones in the manuscript from the Vinayaka Temple."

Sharvil's brow furrowed in concentration as he studied the symbols. "You're right," he confirmed.

They reached a room where manuscripts, preserved in glass cabinets, lay waiting. Anika's fingers danced over one such manuscript with symbols, the words, written in ancient script, barely legible.

Sharvil whispered to Anika, "I hope the manuscripts are in better shape than Mr Sharma. But what do they mean?"

She shushed him, her eyes already wide with anticipation.

"Can you read this?" she whispered to Sharvil.

He squinted, "It looks like old Sanskrit, but I can barely make out the words. You are a Sanskrit scholar, you should be able to read this."

Seeing their confusion, the caretaker offered his expertise, though his eyesight wasn't perfect either. "This verse here speaks of... a 'sacred tree' and a 'silver stream'. I don't know. But I think that might be your next destination."

Thrilled, Anika exclaimed, "We should find this tree! It might lead to more clues."

"I haven't personally visited, but I can recall some clues from memory that might be helpful. However, the local folklore holds much more information," Mr Sharma explained.

After thanking Mr Sharma, the duo set out, their hearts again filled with anticipation.

Reaching the described location wasn't straightforward. Their GPS went haywire, leading them into a thicket where Sharvil almost stepped on a sleeping snake.

"Okay, so nature isn't exactly welcoming us," Anika remarked, her voice shaky.

Brushing off the remnants of the thicket from his shirt, Sharvil replied, "Or maybe nature is trying to tell us we're on the right track."

Hours passed as they hiked, joked and occasionally bickered. Finally, the sound of gushing water reached their ears, and they stumbled upon a beautiful stream, shimmering under the daylight. But to their dismay, there were multiple trees around, none specifically 'sacred' looking.

Anika scratched her head, "Alright, detective Sharvil, which one is our sacred tree?"

Sharvil looked around and pointed to the grandest tree, its branches wide and welcoming. "That one! It's the biggest and looks the oldest."

Without wasting a second, Anika dashed towards it. As she examined its base, she found an engraving, but it wasn't of ancient script. It read: 'Rohit loves Shrishti 2020.'

Sharvil burst out laughing, "Ah, the sacred lovers Rohit and Shrishti!"

Feeling slightly defeated, Anika sighed, "Looks like we were chasing the wrong clue."

Suddenly, an old man (Kalanabha), who was sitting near the stream, called out to them. "You're looking for the ancient tree, aren't you? It's not here. It's on the other side of Mysuru, near the Blue Mountain."

Anika's face brightened with gratitude. "Thank you, sir! We might have been searching for ages without your help!" In her excitement, she hugged Sharvil tightly. Suddenly, everything seemed to freeze around them. By the time they realized it, the old man had disappeared, perhaps into the woods.

As they headed back to their vehicle, Sharvil chuckled, "Sacred tree turned love tree. Today was... unexpectedly eventful."

Anika nudged him, "At least we're moving! Every misadventure is getting us closer to the truth."

Sharvil smiled, taking Anika's hand, "True. And with you, even mistakes seem fun."

Their laughter echoed as they left the stream behind, their bond deepening with each hurdle. The ancient scripts might have misled them this time, but the journey was worth every second.

Local Legends

Sharvil and Anika reached the outskirts of Mysuru, near the famed Blue Mountain. As they moved further into the town, they noticed a busy market square with stalls selling vibrant handicrafts, mouth-watering mysore pak, and colourful silk attire. What caught Anika's attention, however, was a makeshift stage where a local storyteller was narrating tales to an engrossed crowd.

"They could have information about Aditya and Lasya!" Anika whispered excitedly.

Sharvil raised an eyebrow, "Or, it could be another wild goose chase."

They wove through the crowd to get a good spot. The storyteller, an elderly man with a flowing white beard, dressed in a dhoti and kurta, had a voice that carried the weight of years and wisdom. He was narrating a tale of a mischievous god who turned himself into a bird to play pranks on village folk.

Anika leaned over to Sharvil, "Imagine if we took all these tales literally. Life would be so chaotic!"

Sharvil smirked, "Imagine me as a bird, swooping down to steal your samosas."

She chuckled, "Trust you to think of food."

As the tale ended, Anika approached the storyteller, "Baba, we're looking for a legend. About two souls, Aditya and Lasya. Do you know of it?"

The old man stroked his beard, "Ah, a tale from yesteryears! But here, every storyteller has their version."

Before he could proceed, another voice chimed in, "That's not how it goes!" It was a woman, slightly younger, with a twinkle in her eye. "I've got the real tale."

Sharvil whispered, "This is going to be interesting."

The storyteller, not to be outdone, argued, "My version is from my grandfather's grandfather!"

The woman retorted, "And mine's from my grandmother's grandmother. Women have better memories!"

The crowd erupted in laughter. Sensing an opportunity, Anika diplomatically suggested, "Why not have a... story-off? We'd love to hear both versions."

The challenge was accepted.

The old man began, spinning a tale of Aditya and Lasya as mighty warriors from opposing kingdoms, their love story unfolding on a battlefield. "Their arrows crossed, not in enmity but love," he said dramatically.

The woman, introduced as Mala, presented a contrasting picture. In her tale, Aditya was a humble potter, and Lasya was a wandering musician. Their love blossomed over shared songs and crafted clay.

As both tales concluded, the audience was divided over which story was true. The playful debate that ensued was filled with humorous interpretations. Some even came up with their own comical versions, involving mischievous parrots and magical curries.

Sharvil, thoroughly entertained, remarked, "These legends are like a game of Chinese Whispers. Everyone adds their twist."

Anika smiled, "But isn't that the beauty of it? Each version reflects the teller's heart. Perhaps the truth isn't in the exact events but the emotions they convey."

Mala, while offering a souvenir, said, "You know, the exact tales of Aditya and Lasya might differ, but they all revolve around love, trust, and togetherness. That's what you should take from them."

Anika nodded, her eyes soft, "We will. Thank you, Mala."

As they left, the night was brimming with the sounds of distant music, Sharvil remarked, "These local legends definitely remind us that sometimes, the journey and the stories we gather are more precious than the destination."

Here, amidst the local folklore of the land, Sharvil and Anika's own story continued to unfurl, touched with humour, warmth, and with a promise of many more tales to come.

Quantum Queries

Following their entertaining engagement with local legends, Sharvil and Anika found themselves in the serene surroundings of a Mysuru-based university, known for its integration of ancient wisdom with modern science. As they roamed the vast campus, they stumbled upon a sign that read: 'Quantum Mechanics Symposium – All Welcome.'

Sharvil, ever the sceptic, quirked an eyebrow, "You don't suppose they'll discuss the Vedas and quantum entanglement in the same breath, do you?"

Anika, always curious, replied with a sparkle in her eyes, "Only one way to find out!"

Inside the hall, professors, students, and visitors were engrossed in passionate discussions. On stage, a scholar was presenting how ancient scriptures might have hinted at the concept of quantum entanglement.

As they took their seats, Anika leaned towards Sharvil, "Remember the verse we found that hinted at everything being connected?"

Sharvil snorted, "It's not like the verse mentioned quantum physics."

"But isn't it intriguing here?" Anika countered, "Ancient wisdom and modern science potentially converging?"

Before Sharvil could reply, they were interrupted by a chuckle, "You two seem new here." They turned to find an elderly professor with twinkling eyes, Dr Bhushan. Introductions were made, and soon the trio was engrossed in a discussion.

Sharvil, never one to shy away from a debate, posed, "So, you're telling me that our ancestors knew about quantum mechanics?"

Dr Bhushan chuckled, "Not in the way we understand it today, but they had an intuition of the interconnectedness of all things."

Anika's eyes lit up, "Just like Aditya and Lasya being connected across realms!"

Dr Bhushan, intrigued, asked, "Who might they be?"

As Anika narrated their quest, a group of students gathered, drawn by the tale. One of them, a young girl named Rhea, argued, "It sounds poetic, but quantum mechanics doesn't deal with poetry."

Sharvil smirked, "Finally, someone speaking sense."

Anika shot him a playful glare, then addressed Rhea, "But isn't there beauty in science too? The idea that particles, separated by vast distances, can affect each other – doesn't that sound poetic?"

Another student, Arvind, chimed in, "It's more complex than that. But it's interesting to consider how ancient thought might align with this. That too when they had no scientifically advance machines to calculate and measure, or see and observe the quantum happenings."

The debate turned light-hearted, with students playfully miming 'entangled' dance moves and joking about being 'teleported' to the campus canteen.

As the evening deepened, Dr Bhushan shared tales of scholars from eras past, who debated similar conundrums, adding his own humorous anecdotes.

Dr Bhushan continued, explaining a concept from Bucke's Cosmic Consciousness. He discerned three forms, or degrees, of consciousness:

1. Simple consciousness, possessed by both animals and mankind.
2. Self-consciousness, possessed by mankind, which includes thought, reason, and imagination.
3. Cosmic consciousness, a higher form of consciousness than that possessed by the ordinary man. It's like a larger reservoir of consciousness that manifests itself in the minds of men and remains intact even after an individual passes away. It might retain traces of an individual's life history.

He concluded, "While we may not have all the answers, it's these questions that drive us forward. And sometimes, the journey of questioning is more enlightening than the answer."

Sharvil, with feigned exasperation, remarked, "I came for answers, not more questions!"

Anika laughed, nudging him to keep mum.

The symposium concluded with Dr Bhushan gifting them an old book, its pages filled with more queries than answers. "For your journey," he smiled.

Outside, under a blanket of stars, Sharvil admitted, "You know, maybe there's some truth in what you're saying. These ancient verses, quantum theories, they're different paths to the same truth."

Anika squeezed his hand, "The truth of connection. Between us, the world, and the universe, something like cosmic consciousness does exist."

Dr Bhushan turned to Anika and asked, "So, where to next?"

Anika replied, "Himalayas."

Dr Bhushan suggested, "You should visit the Matangeshwara Temple in Khajuraho. There are some ancient Persian scripts inscribed there. Maybe you'll find something interesting."

Revelation at the Ruins

Sharvil and Anika travelled to the warm, sunny ruins of Khajuraho, where ancient temples like Kandariya Mahadeva shared stories of love, reverence and dedication. While exploring the detailed carvings, Anika felt drawn to a specific temple, the Matangeshwara Temple, which was a bit secluded from the main path.

Sharvil noticed Anika's trance-like state. "Hey, daydreamer! Where are you off to?"

Anika, her eyes reflecting a deep sense of familiarity, murmured, "There must be something. Something about Aditya and Lasya."

The temple they approached was adorned with sculptures portraying various stages of love – from the initial shyness, playful courtship, and deepening affection, to eternal commitment. Among these sculptures, one caught Anika's undivided attention. It depicted a royal couple, their gazes locked, their hands intertwined, and an ethereal aura connecting their souls.

"This... this is Aditya and Lasya, and see here, the same symbol too" Anika whispered.

Sharvil, though sceptical, couldn't deny the uncanny resemblance between the depicted couple and the descriptions from the manuscript. "It might be a coincidence," he said, but his voice lacked conviction.

"They were royalty!" Anika exclaimed, piecing together fragments from the verses they'd translated.

As the day turned to evening, they met a local guide named Deepak. He eagerly shared stories about the temple's history. "This temple," he began enthusiastically, "is different. While other temples have different stories, this one is all about a prince who fell in love with a commoner who was known for her dancing." These tales were written on the temple walls in Persian. "Maybe he's your Aditya," Deepak suggested, though he told them that he couldn't be sure.

Sharvil leaned forward, eager for more. "Please, go on," he urged.

Deepak settled himself on the temple's steps, motioning for them to join him. "Prince Aditya was a courageous warrior, while Lasya was a village dancer. Their paths crossed during a village celebration, and it was love at first sight. However, their love faced challenges, not only because of their different social statuses but also due to political tensions."

Anika sighed softly, "Yet, they seem so peaceful as if nothing could disrupt their love."

Deepak smiled warmly, "Despite all the challenges, their love remained strong, showing everyone that love has no limits. And to honour their love, this temple was built."

Sharvil joked, "So, it's like a Bollywood movie plot, right?"

Anika nudged him gently, "Come on, Sharvil. This story has depth, just like our journey."

Deepak chuckled, "Legend has it that those who seek Aditya and Lasya's blessings here often find true love."

Sharvil pretended to be surprised, glancing at Anika, "Is that why we're here?"

She laughed, "Well, a little blessing couldn't hurt, could it?"

As the sun set over the ancient ruins, Sharvil and Anika sat beside the temple, taking in its stories. Sharvil, in a rare moment of honesty, confessed, "You know, Anika, I joined this journey out of curiosity. But now, it means more to me. Maybe... I don't know..."

Anika smiled, her eyes shining, "Aditya and Lasya's tale may be old, but its message is timeless. Just like us. Maybe... I don't know..."

To the Himalayas

"Now, let's go to the Himalayas!" Anika exclaimed the next morning, inspired by a dream where Aditya and Lasya seemed to be amidst snow-capped mountains.

Sharvil yawned, stretching his arms, "Now to freezing mountains? Anika, you really know how to vacation."

She rolled her eyes, "Come on, Sharvil! The mountains are calling!"

He chuckled, "Oh, is that so? Did they send a text or was it a missed call?"

The train journey from Khajuraho to Srinagar was an episode in itself. They'd mistakenly booked seats in separate compartments.

"I can't believe you booked our seats separately!" Anika chided.

Sharvil defended, "It's an adventure, remember? Actually, I booked the tickets in Tatkal so the seats are random allocation."

As the train rattled on, they shuttled between compartments, sharing snacks, and jokes, and making new friends. An elderly lady mistook them for a honeymooning couple, much to their amusement.

She winked at Anika, "He's a good catch. Don't let him go."

Sharvil, overhearing, smirked, "See? I'm approved by the elderly community."

As they settled into their hotel room in Srinagar, at night, Sharvil turned to Anika with a hopeful look. "Anika, what do you think about visiting Gulmarg tomorrow?"

Anika noticed Sharvil's excitement and smiled. "Gulmarg? Why there?"

Sharvil chuckled. "Well, it's a beautiful honeymoon destination with great skiing opportunities. Plus, it's not too far from here."

Anika raised an eyebrow. "But we're not on a honeymoon, Sharvil."

Sharvil laughed. "I know, I know. But it'll be fun to explore the place together, just as friends."

Anika nodded, warming up to the idea (mostly due to Sharvil excitement in his eyes). "Well, if you're that thrilled about it, then count me in! A day in Gulmarg sounds like it could be fun."

With their plans set, they looked forward to their upcoming day trip to Gulmarg, ready to explore its beauty and experience the excitement of skiing on the snowy slopes.

The next day, they hired a car to Gulmarg. As Anika and Sharvil journeyed through the beautiful countryside on their way to Gulmarg, they couldn't contain their excitement. The countryside was filled with pretty flowers and green trees, making Anika's eyes shine with joy. Sharvil smiled at her, feeling happy to see her so excited.

As they travelled, they passed by the Mirung Apple Orchard, where Anika couldn't resist picking a juicy apple. They also visited Chokhar Hill, where they saw amazing views.

Finally, they reached Drung Waterfall, the last stop of the day. Drung Waterfall is a famous place known for its stunning waterfall, caves, an old temple, Ferozpora Nalla, and a hydropower plant. The waterfall flows fast, surrounded by tall pine trees and small hills.

As they reached, the sound of the rushing water was loud, but it was also very soothing. Anika and Sharvil stood together, looking at the waterfall in awe.

Anika felt really happy and excited. When she looked at Sharvil, she saw that he was looking at her with a loving expression. Their eyes met, and for a moment, they felt like the waterfall had frozen like it does in winter.

Speechless with emotion, Anika took a deep breath. Sharvil reached out and gently brushed her silky, shiny hair away from her face. Anika felt his touch and couldn't help but lean into his embrace. It felt like they were the only two people in the world.

They hugged each other tightly, feeling the warmth of their love. Anika felt safe and happy in Sharvil's arms, and she didn't want the moment to end. Eventually, they let go and smiled at each other, knowing that their bond was going strong and special. They were excited to see what the future held for them.

They decided to make the most of their time and planned an action-packed day in Gulmarg. Their first stop was Kangdori, a bowl-shaped valley nestled between Gulmarg and Apharwat. Kangdori served as the starting point for the famous gondola ride, a must-do activity in Gulmarg. As they ascended in the gondola, they marvelled at the stunning views of the valley below. Anika couldn't help but gasp at the breathtaking scenery, while Sharvil eagerly pointed out the snow-covered peaks in the distance.

As Anika and Sharvil geared up for their skiing adventure in Gulmarg, excitement and nervousness mingled in the air. Anika adjusted her goggles while Sharvil struggled to put on his ski boots, his face contorted in concentration.

"Are you sure we're ready for this?" Anika asked, her voice tinted with apprehension.

Sharvil flashed her a confident smile. "Of course, we'll be fine! What's the worst that could happen?"

Famous last words, Anika thought to herself as they made their way to the ski slopes. The instructor, a seasoned pro with a mischievous twinkle in his eye, greeted them with a hearty laugh.

"Welcome, welcome! Ready to hit the slopes?" he exclaimed, clapping Sharvil on the back with enough force to nearly send him tumbling.

Anika shot Sharvil a playful smirk. "I hope you're more graceful on skis than you are on solid ground."

Sharvil stuck out his tongue in response, earning a chuckle from the instructor. "We'll see about that!"

As they began their lesson, Anika quickly discovered that skiing was much harder than it looked. She wobbled and teetered on her skis, her arms flailing wildly as she tried to maintain her balance. Sharvil, on the other hand, seemed to take to it like a natural, effortlessly gliding down the slopes with a grin plastered on his face.

Anika couldn't help but feel a twinge of envy as she watched him. "How are you so good at this?" she grumbled, struggling to keep up.

Sharvil shrugged nonchalantly. "Beginner's luck, I guess."

But luck seemed to have abandoned Anika as she moved down the slope, narrowly avoiding a collision with a group of beginners. She let out a squeal of terror, flapping her arms like a startled bird as she tried to regain her balance.

"Watch out!" she shouted, sending Sharvil veering off course to avoid her.

The instructor rushed over, his laughter echoing in the crisp mountain air. "Looks like we've got a couple of comedians on our hands!"

Despite her initial struggles, Anika refused to give up. With grit and determination, she pushed herself to keep going, determined to conquer the slopes no matter what. Slowly but surely, she began to improve, her confidence growing with each turn.

As they reached the bottom of the slope, panting and exhilarating, Anika couldn't help but laugh at the absurdity of it all. "Well, that was certainly an experience!"

Sharvil grinned, his eyes sparkling with mischief. "One we won't be forgetting anytime soon!"

And as they stood there, catching their breath and basking in the glow of their accomplishment, Anika felt a surge of affection for Sharvil. Leaning in, she pressed a soft kiss to his cheek, her heart fluttering with joy.

"Thanks for being my ski buddy," she whispered, her voice filled with warmth.

Sharvil's grin widened, his cheeks flushing with delight. "Anytime, Anika. Anytime."

After their adrenaline-filled adventure, they retreated to a cosy café to warm up with hot chocolate and reminisce about their day.

As night fell, they realized it was too late to return to Srinagar and decided to spend the night in Gulmarg. They found a charming guesthouse nestled amidst the snow-covered hills and settled in for the night, their hearts full of joy and gratitude for the unforgettable experiences they had shared. As they drifted off to sleep, they knew that Gulmarg had stolen a piece of their hearts forever.

Chapter 3
Introspection

Mountain Misadventures

The next morning in the Himalayas greeted Anika and Sharvil with a sheet of white mist covering their lodge window. Anika, ever the enthusiast, was the first to rise, her nose pressed against the cold glass, eagerly trying to catch a glimpse of the world outside.

Sharvil groaned from beneath layers of blankets. "It's too early and too cold. Five more minutes..."

Anika pulled the blankets away, "Come on, sleepyhead! The mountains await!"

The chill of the room hit Sharvil instantly. "Okay, maybe ten more minutes," he murmured, burrowing deeper into the mattress. After a couple of hours, they started and reached Pulwama by taxi.

Their first order of business was to acclimatize to the thin air. The lodge manager, an old Tibetan named Tenzin, suggested a short trek.

"Walk slow, breathe deep," he advised. "And don't run, even if you're being chased by a yak."

Sharvil laughed, "Being chased by a yak? Is that a common occurrence here?"

Tenzin winked, "You never know with the mountain winds."

The trek was harder than either had imagined. Every few steps felt like a marathon.

"I feel like I've aged forty years," Sharvil puffed, clutching his side, "And I think my lungs are staging a protest."

Anika, equally winded, teased, "Thought you were fit, Mr Gym Enthusiast?"

Their playful banter was interrupted when a herd of yaks blocked their path. Anika's eyes widened in delight, but Sharvil, recalling Tenzin's advice, looked apprehensive.

"What now?" he whispered. Before Anika could answer, one curious yak approached Sharvil, sniffing him and then taking a liking to his scarf. In seconds, the yak started pulling Sharvil along.

"Help!" Sharvil squeaked.

Anika, suppressing her laughter, called out, "Stay calm! Maybe it thinks you're part of its herd!"

With the help of a local shepherd, they managed to disentangle Sharvil from the yak.

Once safe, Anika couldn't hold back. "I can't believe you got kidnapped by a yak!"

Sharvil, feigning indignation, said, "At least, he had good taste. This scarf is designer."

In evening, as they sat around a campfire, Anika leaned into Sharvil, "You know, these misadventures, the laughter, the moments... they're making me feel special."

Sharvil nodded, wrapping an arm around her, "It's like the universe is throwing challenges our way, testing us, and we're just laughing in its face."

The mountains, with all its challenges, became a metaphor for life. It wasn't about avoiding missteps but how one reacted to them. And with each other's company, Anika and Sharvil were finding joy in the unexpected.

Cave Chronicles

The Himalayas, with their vast expanse, were both a beauty and a mystery. Amidst their trekking adventures, the duo came across an intriguing mention of Gufkral cave located at Banmir village in the Tral Tehsil of the Pulwama District, known for its ancient inscriptions and 'Anand of Kashmir'.

The day continued with them asking locals about the cave's whereabouts. An old, wise-looking woman named Doma shared tales she had heard in her youth. "The cave you seek has walls that talk," she said cryptically, her eyes distant, remembering. "But it won't easily reveal itself. You should take a lantern with you."

Sharvil, ever the sceptic, chuckled, "Walls that talk? Maybe they chit-chat with the yaks?"

Anika shot him a look, "Maybe it's metaphorical! Stories, history... you know!"

With a vague map drawn on a piece of old parchment and Doma's words as their only guide, they set off.

As they neared the cave's supposed location, they faced their first challenge: a narrow ledge leading up to a cliff. A misstep could lead to a tumble into the rushing waters below.

Sharvil gulped. "You sure about this?"

Anika smirked, "Scared? It's just like a tightrope walk, but, you know, with a potential deadly plunge."

He rolled his eyes, "Oh, just that? Why didn't you say so earlier?"

Taking a deep breath, Sharvil made his way, arms flailing comically for balance. Anika followed, giggling at his antics. Both breathed sighs of relief upon reaching the other side.

Their next challenge was a steep, near-vertical climb. Anika tried to scale it but slid back down, landing on her rear. Sharvil's attempt wasn't any better. After a few attempts, they were just covered in snow.

"I think the universe is having a little too much fun at our expense," Anika remarked, brushing off the snow.

Sharvil nodded, "And I'm starting to think these walls better have a lot to say after all this effort."

Just when they were about to give up, a group of young village kids chanced upon them. With amused grins, they showed the duo an easier route they had completely missed.

With reddened faces, Anika and Sharvil finally stood at the cave's entrance. It was more magnificent than they had imagined, with a serene aura.

The cave looked dark and scary against the white snow all around. The sky above was dark, but there was a strange light that made everything look mysterious.

Even though it was cold and windy, there was something exciting about the cave. It felt like there could be hidden treasures waiting inside. Anika and Sharvil felt a mix of fear and excitement as they looked at the cave entrance.

Despite feeling a little scared, they were curious to explore the cave. They wondered what they might find hidden in its icy depths. With their hearts pounding, they took small steps into the darkness.

Inside the cave, it was cold and quiet. But there was also a strange beauty to it. Icy formations hung from the ceiling, shining like diamonds in the dim light. Anika and Sharvil couldn't help but marvel at the sight.

As they ventured further into the cave, their fear started to fade away. Instead, they felt amazed by the wonders around them. The walls seemed to hold secrets of the ancient world, and they were eager to uncover them.

Guided by the light of their lantern, Anika and Sharvil explored deeper into the cave.

As they ventured in, they were greeted by walls covered in ancient inscriptions and drawings. Sharvil attempted to decipher them but ended up narrating a comically twisted version of events.

Anika laughed, "Really? So, according to you, this stick figure is a king who loved dancing with yaks?"

Sharvil grinned, "You never know! History is weird."

They spent hours in the cave, interpreting the inscriptions, making up silly stories, and sharing genuine moments of wonder.

Sharvil looked at the wall, trying to make out the faint inscriptions. "You know, at this point, I half expect these to be dinner recipes from a thousand years ago."

Anika chuckled, "Given our translation track record, it might very well be."

Venturing further inside, the cave's solemn air enveloped them. And there it was – the mural, expansive and rich in detail, narrating a divine dance of Shiva and Shakti. Their figures, intricate and expressive, were surrounded by various symbols, animals, and celestial beings.

Anika, ever the enthusiast, pulled out her notebook, jotting down immediate observations. "Look at Shiva's hand, the way it's pointed. And Shakti's feet, the dance pose she's in."

Sharvil leaned in, squinting, "You mean the way she seems to be stomping on his foot? Was this the divine version of 'You stepped on my toes' at a dance?"

She swatted him lightly, "Be serious!"

Deciphering the mural was tricky. Anika noticed a snake around Shiva's neck and a crescent moon on his head. "Maybe the snake means... um, starting anew? Or is time passing? And the moon... um, his calm side?"

Sharvil joked, "Maybe he just liked fancy stuff. Check out that trident. Definitely makes a statement."

A saint with a white beard, resembling the old man Anika had encountered near an old tree in Karnataka, overheard their conversation. He approached them with a smile. "Young ones, would you like to know the real story behind the mural?"

Anika nodded eagerly, "Yes, please. Before we make up a story about Shiva and Shakti entering a divine fashion show."

The saint chuckled, "So, the prophecy was true after all," the saint chuckled, eyeing Anika and Sharvil as they pondered over the mural in their own peculiar way. "That one day, a lovely couple would grace this place and interpret the murals in the most unconventional manner."

Anika glanced at Sharvil with a grin, "Well, we do have a knack for adding our unique touch to everything."

Sharvil nodded, playing along, "Absolutely! Who needs traditional interpretations when you have our creative flair?"

The saint laughed heartily, "Indeed, it's refreshing to see such a... unique approach to ancient art. But perhaps, let me offer some insights before you turn this divine story into a comedy show."

The saint then delved into the deeper meanings behind each element of the mural. He pointed to the snake, explaining how it symbolized the latent energy dormant within every individual, waiting to awaken. Next, he gestured to the moon, signifying the cyclical nature of time and Shiva's mastery over it. Lastly, he spoke of the dance of Shiva and Shakti, representing the cosmic dance of creation and destruction, illustrating the eternal balance between masculine and feminine energies.

Sharvil, always curious yet respectful, raised an eyebrow, "So, no fashion show then?"

The saint chuckled, "No, young man. But their dance is far more profound than mere steps. It's the rhythm of the universe, the harmony that maintains balance in all things.

The saint then led them deeper into the cave, where they discovered a magnificent statue of Nataraja, the dancing form of Lord Shiva. Beside the statue, there was a flickering diya and various sacred items, adding to the mystical ambience of the cave.

"In this Nataraja sculpture," the saint began, "Shiva is depicted as the source of all movement within the cosmos. His dance, represented by the arch of flames, accompanies the dissolution of the universe at the end of an eon.

Anika and Sharvil listened intently as the saint continued to explain the symbolism behind the statue. "The ring of cosmic fire surrounding Shiva's dance represents time, which destroys everything in its path. Within this cosmic circle, the Nataraja sculpture portrays Shiva as the source of all movement in the universe. His cosmic dance, depicted by the arch of flames, signifies the end of the universe. This dance is said to have taken place in Chidambaram, a significant Shaiva centre in South India, known as both the centre of the universe and the human heart.

In the sculpture, Shiva's gestures symbolize five activities: creation (represented by the drum), protection (shown by the "fear-not" pose of the hand), destruction (depicted by the fire), embodiment (seen in the foot planted on the ground), and release (shown by the foot held aloft).

Aside from the Nataraja dance, Shiva's other dances include the wild tandava, performed on cremation grounds with his consort Devi, and the graceful Lasya, performed on Mount Kailas in the evening before the assembly of gods. Dance forms have two aspects, Tandava (Masculine) and Lasya (Feminine).

Sharvil nodded, fascinated by the profound symbolism. "So, the dance of Nataraja represents the rhythm of creation and destruction, the balance that maintains harmony in the universe?"

The saint smiled, "Exactly! And each element of the dance holds deep meaning. Let me elaborate. Shiva's drum symboliszs creation, originating as sound, as vibration. It's like the rhythm of existence itself."

Anika's eyes sparkled with curiosity. "And what about the gestures of protection and destruction?"

"The gestures represent the balance between creation and destruction," the saint explained. "Shiva holds the power of both, signifying the eternal cycle of life and death."

As they gazed at the statue in awe, the saint continued further, "Nataraja's foot resting on a dwarf symbolizes his control over the human ego and spiritual illusion. And his uplifted leg represents grace, leading souls to liberation from worldly bondage."

Anika and Sharvil exchanged a look of wonder, marvelling at the depth of Hindu mythology. "It's incredible how mythology, religion, and science intersect," Anika remarked.

Sharvil nodded, "Yes, it's like a seamless blend of ancient wisdom and modern understanding."

As they left the cave, the echoes of the saint's words lingered in their minds, leaving them with a newfound appreciation for the cosmic dance of Nataraja and its profound significance in Hindu philosophy.

As they continued on their path, Sharvil nudged Anika, "You do realize that from now on, every dance I see, I'll be wondering about the cosmic implications, right?"

Anika laughed, "Only if you promise to refrain from stepping on my toes."

Their laughter paralleled a harmonious tune amidst the Himalayan silence, a reminder of the balance they were finding, not just in ancient murals but within themselves and with each other.

Sharvil's Quantum Quandary

Their final stop was the Lamayuru Monastery, a peaceful place nestled among the snowy peaks of Ladakh. Anika and Sharvil had heard stories of monks who could supposedly connect with something called the 'quantum field' through meditation, so they thought they'd give it a try. Sharvil, being interested in science, found the idea intriguing.

As they arrived, they were met by Lama Tenzin at the gate, an old monk who seemed to have a knowing smile like he was already aware of their visit. "Ah, seekers of the quantum realm," Lama Tenzin greeted them warmly. "You wish to connect with the field that binds everything, don't you?"

Anika nodded eagerly. "We've heard that the state can be achieved through deep meditation. I'm quite familiar with the practice, but my friend Sharvil here..." she paused, glancing at Sharvil with a mischievous smirk.

Sharvil scoffed playfully. "I'm just scientifically curious. Besides, how hard can it be? Sit, breathe, think of nothing."

Lama Tenzin chuckled. "Very well, let's begin."

The trio sat down in the monastery's meditation hall, a serene room filled with the soft glow of butter lamps and the subtle scent of incense. Anika eased into a meditative state, her breathing steady and face serene.

Sharvil, on the other hand, was a study in comedic discomfort. He shifted his weight, tried crossing his legs in various configurations, and frowned in concentration.

After what felt like hours to Sharvil (but was actually only ten minutes), he whispered desperately to Lama Tenzin, "Is it normal to feel an itch on the nose?"

The old monk suppressed a smile. "It's just the mind playing tricks. Let it pass."

Another ten minutes in, Sharvil's eyes popped open. "I think I've got it! I'm feeling... something! A tingling sensation."

Lama Tenzin, with saintly patience, responded, "That's just your foot falling asleep. Adjust your position."

As Anika meditated deeply, Sharvil's internal monologue was an amusingly chaotic mess:

Alright, focus on breathing. In... out... in... out... Oh, I wonder if we'll have momos for lunch. No! Focus! Think of nothing. Absolutely nothing... Except maybe grilled momos. Do they make those?

His stomach growled audibly, echoing in the silent hall. Lama Tenzin's eyes crinkled in silent laughter.

After a deep meditation session guided by Lama Tenzin, Anika felt a sense of peace wash over her. As the monk gently touched her forehead with his thumb, something extraordinary happened. Anika's mind was transported to another realm, where she caught a glimpse of herself existing in a different reality. It was a surreal experience, leaving her both bewildered and intrigued.

An hour later, Anika emerged from her meditation, refreshed and calm. She looked at Sharvil, who was now lying flat on his back, staring at the ceiling. "Did you connect with the quantum field?" she teased. She didn't say anything about the glimpse as she thought Sharvil would laugh at her.

Sharvil groaned. "I connected with my stomach and my aching back. Does that count?"

Lama Tenzin, ever gracious, chimed in, "Meditation, like any other practice, takes time. Some are natural, while others, like our friend Sharvil here, might need a... unique approach."

Sharvil sat up, intrigued. "What do you suggest?"

"How about a walking meditation? Or even better, a dancing one. The universe doesn't demand the stillness of the body. It celebrates movement and energy, much like the quantum field your mind just has to be calm."

Later that day, in the monastery's courtyard, the sight was one for the ages. Anika, Lama Tenzin, and a few amused monks watched as Sharvil attempted a 'quantum dance' – a blend of erratic movements, punctuated with moments of stillness.

Every time he felt embarrassed, Sharvil remembered Lama Tenzin's words: The universe celebrates movement. And move, he did. By the end, he was out of breath but undeniably joyful.

When they were leaving Lama Tenzin gave them a scroll and said, "Keep it with you. It may help you further."

Anika saw the same symbol on that scroll too. Without saying a word she accepted it with a smile.

As they left the monastery, Anika teased, "So, Mr Scientist, how was your quantum experience?"

Sharvil smiled, "Let's just say I've discovered that the universe has a sense of humour. And it's laughing with me, not at me."

The two friends continued their journey, taking with them memories of dancing amidst the Himalayas.

Aditya and Lasya's Lament

On the final day of their stay in the Himalayas, Anika and Sharvil, having learned a lot about themselves, decided to delve again into the story of Aditya and Lasya, the ancient lovers whose tales had brought them to this point.

They sat by a campfire and Anika pulled out the ancient scrolls they had collected on their journey, and Sharvil leaned in, curious.

"According to these scrolls," Anika began, "Aditya and Lasya were not just ordinary lovers. Their love was the kind that could move mountains, change rivers' courses, and alter destinies."

Now Anika and Sharvil had a better understanding of the words of the manuscript and scrolls.

Sharvil raised an eyebrow, intrigued. "Tell me more."

Anika took a deep breath. "Aditya was a prince from a hidden village Sambala, set to inherit his father's vast kingdom, while Lasya was a commoner, a dancer who performed in the village square. From the moment Aditya laid eyes on Lasya, he was spellbound. Her grace, her energy, the spark was magnetic."

Sharvil smirked, "Sounds like a Bollywood plot."

Anika nudged him playfully. "Don't interrupt. Their love story was anything but ordinary."

She continued, "Every evening, Aditya would sneak out of the palace to watch Lasya dance, and over time, the two grew close. They would meet in secret, under the cover of night, sharing stories and dreams."

"One evening, as they sat by the river, Aditya gifted Lasya a pendant – a beautiful piece with a blue stone, said to be as deep as the ocean. Lasya, in return, gave him a handcrafted anklet she wore during her dances. It was their promise to each other – symbols of an unbreakable bond."

"Yes, indeed," Sharvil leaned in, "But every love story has a twist. What was theirs?"

Anika sighed, "The king, Aditya's father, had other plans for his son. He had arranged for Aditya to marry a princess from a neighbouring Agartha kingdom. This alliance was crucial for the peace and prosperity of their land.

Sharvil, engrossed in the story, whispered, "What did he do?"

"Aditya approached Lasya with a heavy heart and told her about his father's plans. He expected tears and anger, but Lasya just smiled sadly. She understood the weight of his responsibilities."

"She whispered, 'If our love is true, it will find its way back, no matter the lifetimes or barriers.'

"As the eve of his wedding approached, Aditya found himself restless, his mind consumed by haunting thoughts. Unable to ignore the tug at his heart, he slipped away from the grandeur of the palace, seeking solace in the quiet embrace of the night. His footsteps, soft against the cool marble floors, led him to Lasya, the one person who could understand the turmoil within him.

"With a gentle touch, Aditya reached out to Lasya, his eyes searching hers for solace. At that moment, words seemed unnecessary as they stood beneath the soft moonlight, their hearts beating in unison. With a silent understanding, they began to dance, each movement is an indication to the depth of their connection.

"As they twirled and swayed, the world around them faded into insignificance, leaving only the rhythm of their footsteps and the whispered promises of their hearts. In the tender embrace of the night, they found refuge in each other's arms, their souls entwined in a dance of love and longing.

"As the first light of dawn painted the sky with hues of pink and gold, reality came crashing back with a bittersweet finality. Reluctantly, Aditya and Lasya parted ways, their hearts heavy with the weight of impending separation. Yet, even as they bid each other farewell, a glimmer of hope remained alive within them, a silent promise that their love would endure, transcending time and reality.

"In that fleeting moment beneath the moonlit sky, Aditya and Lasya had shared a love that was pure and timeless, a love that would linger in their hearts long after the night had faded into memory. And as they walked away from each other, their souls intertwined, they knew that no matter where life may lead them, their love would always find its way back home."

Sharvil's eyes glistened, "That's heart-breaking. What happened to Lasya?"

Anika replied, "Lasya continued to dance, pouring her love, her pain, and her hopes into every performance. The village spoke of her dances being so poignant that even the heavens wept. And Aditya? He fulfilled his duties as a king, a husband, and a father. But every night, he'd gaze at the moon, remembering their final dance."

"They say," Anika continued with a tremor in her voice, "that the pendant and anklet are still out there, waiting to be reunited, just like Aditya and Lasya."

Sharvil looked deep into the fire. "You know, their story, it's more than just a love story. It's about sacrifices, understanding, and hope."

Anika nodded, "Yes, and maybe, just maybe, our journey is somehow tied to theirs. Perhaps we're meant to find those tokens of love."

The two of them sat quietly, the fire crackling beside them as the chilly breeze whispered stories of love and dreams. They realized that their adventure had only just begun. Now, it wasn't just about unravelling ancient verses but also about discovering the true meaning of love and the sacrifices it required.

Anika took a big breath, "You know, before this trip, I had these walls up around me. They were supposed to keep me safe, to stop me from getting hurt again. But now, they feel like they're falling apart."

Sharvil sat up, looking at her with kindness, "Why did you build those walls, Anika?"

She paused, chewing on her lip. "I guess it was because of things that happened before. Disappointments. I just didn't want to feel weak or hurt again."

Sharvil's face softened. "Anika, walls can protect you, but they also keep out the good stuff. Being vulnerable isn't a bad thing. It means you're alive, you're real, and you can love and learn."

A tear slid down Anika's cheek, "Thanks, dear. This journey, our talks, even our little fights, they're helping me to trust again, to open up."

Sharvil wiped her tears gently, "And thanks to you too, for showing me the beauty in simple things. Like this snowball fight, it's been amazing."

They shared a smile, feeling warm inside despite the chill around them. As the sun started to set, painting the snow golden, they got up, hand in hand, ready to keep going, their connection stronger than ever.

As they talked on the snow-covered ground, they looked up at the vast blue sky, taking in the peacefulness of the moment. It felt like an invitation to reflect on their journey and themselves.

Finding Lasya's Verse

Sharvil and Anika had spent days rummaging through ancient scriptures, seeking something – anything – that might connect them further to Lasya and Aditya's story. Their journey so far had been a mix of deep revelations, laughs, and an ever-deepening bond.

One chilly morning, with the first rays of the sun painting the Himalayan peaks in gold, they sat in their camp. Anika was skimming through a particularly old-looking manuscript, her brow furrowed in concentration, while Sharvil wrestled with a can of berries, trying to pry it open without a can opener.

As Anika read out loud, her voice blending with the ambient sounds of nature, Sharvil muttered to himself, "Why do they make these cans so darn difficult to open? Need a Ph.D. in can-ology or something..."

Anika, not really listening to Sharvil's grumbling, suddenly stopped mid-sentence. "Wait... this might be it!" she exclaimed.

"What, a can opener?" Sharvil asked, his attention still focused on his stubborn can.

"No, you goof! Lasya's verse!" She read aloud:

In love's dance, two souls entwine,
The masculine moon, the feminine sunshine
Where Aditya's strength does brightly glow,
Lasya's grace makes the rivers flow.

A silence fell between them. It was as if the universe itself had paused to acknowledge the gravity of their discovery.

Then, breaking the silence, Sharvil asked, "So, does this mean Lasya was the sunshine to Aditya's moon?"

Anika laughed, nodding. "Looks like it. It's beautiful, isn't it?"

"Yeah," Sharvil mused, "Like berries and cocoa. Separately good, but together... actually, that's a terrible combo. Forget I said that."

Anika chuckled. "Only you could find a way to link ancient love verses to berries and cocoa."

"But in all seriousness," Sharvil said, a smile playing on his lips, "It's moments like these when we unearth pieces of the past that I feel a weird mix of excitement and reverence."

Anika nodded, "It's like we're detectives, but instead of solving crimes, we're piecing together tales of love and wisdom from aeons ago."

"And using modern slang to interpret them," Sharvil added with a grin.

"That too," Anika laughed.

Love and Entanglement

The discovery of Lasya's verse had added a new layer to their quest. As the campfire crackled, its warm light contrasting with the deepening cold, Anika wrapped a shawl around herself.

"You know," she began, her gaze fixed on the vast heavens above, "the ancients believed that stars were souls. Souls that had lived, loved, and returned to the cosmos."

Sharvil, roasting some marshmallows on the fire, glanced at her. "So, in a way, the sky is like a canvas of countless love stories?"

Anika smiled, "Maybe. Stories that span eons, like Aditya and Lasya's."

Sharvil, turning his marshmallow stick, said hesitantly, "You know, this journey... with you... it's changed me. I came here, sceptical of these old tales and now, I'm not just a believer, but a part of it."

Anika turned to face him, her eyes searching his. "What do you mean?"

He took a deep breath, "I mean, amidst these ancient stories, I've discovered a new one. Our story."

She blinked, surprised. "Sharvil..."

"I know, I know," he interrupted, chuckling lightly. "Mr Sceptic, always poking fun... but never taking anything seriously. But this... this feels different." He looked into her eyes. "Remember quantum entanglement?"

She nodded, a slow smile forming on her pink supple lips, "When two particles become interconnected, the state of one instantly influences the state of the other, no matter the distance."

"Exactly. It's like... even though they're apart, they're forever connected. They're a part of a whole." He paused, taking a moment to gather his thoughts. "I feel that with you. It's as if our souls have become entangled, intertwined in this journey, in this story. Maybe one day, string theory will make sense of all this, or at least show us that you and I are connected by invisible strings."

Anika's heart raced, the warmth in her chest contrasting with the cold around her. "Sharvil, I... I feel it too. This connection. I've been trying to find the right words, but I guess you beat me to it with your quantum analogy."

He grinned, "Well, there had to be some use of my science background on this trip."

They both laughed, the sound reverberating in the vastness around them.

Then, Anika, with a twinkle in her eyes, added, "So, are you saying we're like those entangled particles? Forever influencing each other's state?"

Sharvil nodded, "Yes, and like them, even when we're apart, we are connected."

Their hands reached out, fingers entwining, mirroring the entanglement they spoke of.

The night deepened, but the warmth between them grew. The journey that had started as an exploration of ancient tales had become their own love story.

Chapter 4
Revelation

A Decision

Back in Mumbai, at her apartment, Anika took a big breath. "Finding these stories has been special. Shouldn't we share them?" she asked Sharvil.

Sharvil nodded, "I've been thinking about that. How do we do it? Maybe a book? Or a video?"

Anika's eyes sparkled, "Let's do both! Picture this: Aditya and Lasya's story mixed with ours. It's like blending the past and the present."

Sharvil grinned, "I can already imagine the title, 'Entangled: Love Across Time'. Or something poetic like that."

Laughing, Anika said, "You're always the dramatic one. But yes, let's capture what we've discovered. And imagine the talks and workshops we could do!"

Sharvil got serious, "You know, it's not just about the love story. What we've learned about the universe, the mix of spirituality and science, it could change how we see everything."

Feeling his sincerity, Anika replied, "That's why we need to be careful, and thoughtful. We should talk to experts, work with historians, scientists, and spiritual guides."

Sharvil agreed, "It's more than just telling a story. It's about connecting the ancient with the modern."

They sat quietly, knowing the weight of their decision. Sharing their discoveries was about starting a big conversation, a revival of old wisdom.

As the day faded, Anika gathered their notes. "This is going to be a big job. Translating, explaining, and making it interesting."

Helping her, Sharvil said, "But we've got each other. And our journey to guide us."

She smiled, "You're right. From strangers to... what? Partners-in-crime in this entangled journey?"

He laughed, "Something like that."

The world was waiting to hear their story, and they were ready to share it.

Dr Aryan's Amusement

In the heart of the city was the Chhatrapati Shivaji Maharaj Vastu Sangrahalaya. As an archaeologist and curator, Dr Aryan's office was a fascinating blend of modern design and artefacts. Draped in his tweed jacket and square-framed glasses, he looked every bit the serious academic. But those who knew him were aware of the sparkling mischief in his eyes.

Sharvil and Anika had set up a meeting with him to discuss their findings. As they sat in the waiting room, Anika whispered, "I've heard he's quite a character. Don't be shocked if he's a bit... unconventional."

Sharvil raised an eyebrow.

The secretary gestured them in, and they stepped into an office that felt more like Aladdin's cave. Artefacts, papers, and random trinkets were everywhere. And in the centre, behind a teetering pile of books, sat Dr Aryan.

He looked up, a twinkle in his eye, "Ah, the adventurers! I've been expecting you. My assistant told me about the request. Come."

Sharvil started, "Thank you for meeting us, Dr Aryan. We believe we've made some astonishing discoveries, and—"

Dr Aryan interrupted, "Is it a lost city? Or maybe the fountain of youth? I could use some of that!"

Anika giggled, "No, but perhaps something just as astonishing."

Handing over their findings, photos, and notes, Anika began to explain their journey, the clues, the murals, and the ancient verses. Dr Aryan, looking amused, sifted through the papers.

Sharvil, slightly irritated, remarked, "This is serious research, Doctor."

Dr Aryan glanced up, "Oh, I know. But life is too short to always be serious. The universe has a sense of humour, you know? Always leaves us humans scratching our heads."

Anika, sensing an opening, quipped, "Speaking of the universe, you might enjoy our quantum interpretations."

Dr Aryan leaned back, steepling his fingers. "Ah, the wonders of quantum! You know, I once had a cat named Schrödinger. Or maybe I didn't. He was quite an uncertain fellow."

Sharvil, chuckling, said, "Well, this is more about love and quantum entanglement."

Dr Aryan's face lit up. "Love, now that's the real mystery. You can crack quantum, but love? That's the universe's real puzzle."

Anika, playfully, added, "Perhaps love is the universe's way of having fun at our expense?"

"Ah, Miss Anika! Now you're speaking my language!" Dr Aryan exclaimed. "Let's hear it, then. Tell me about this quantum love."

As Sharvil and Anika explained, Dr Aryan listened, interrupting with quips and jokes, lightening the serious mood. At one point, as Anika showed a mural of Aditya and Lasya,

Dr Aryan remarked, "They look quite dashing. Bollywood, watch out!"

Sharvil, explaining their theories, couldn't help but be infected by Dr Aryan's humour. "And here," Sharvil pointed at a mural, "We believe this represents the cosmic dance of Shiva and Shakti, or maybe they were just practising for a dance competition."

Dr Aryan roared with laughter, "I like you, young man!"

After hours of discussions, debates, and countless jokes, Dr Aryan sat back, looking pensive. "You've done an impressive job. Your findings might rewrite history, and your interpretations, while humorous, have depth."

Anika, relieved, responded, "So, you believe us?"

Dr Aryan smiled warmly, "I believe that every discovery begins with a question and a sense of wonder. You've brought both, and a dash of humour to boot."

Sharvil, looking around the room filled with artefacts, asked, "Where do we go from here, Doctor?"

Dr Aryan winked, "To the world, of course! But first, tea. I've got a Himalayan blend. Or as you might call it, chai latte."

As they laughed and sipped their tea, the room felt like a confluence of the past, the present, and myriad possibilities of the future. Dr Aryan, with his vast knowledge and infectious humour, was the perfect bridge between ancient wisdom and modern interpretations.

Bridging Gaps

In the days that followed, Dr Aryan's office turned into a hub of intellectual hustle and bustle. The archaeologist's initial amusement transformed into genuine enthusiasm. He decided to host a series of seminars, inviting scholars, scientists, and theologians to the museum to discuss the union of quantum physics and ancient scriptures.

Sharvil, with his background in modern science, often found himself dumbfounded by the deep correlations between quantum mechanics and the age-old wisdom from the scriptures. Anika, on the other hand, with her affinity for history and spirituality, was like a fish in water, swimming seamlessly between the past and the present.

The first session started with a scientist named Dr Naina, a woman with a head full of curls and a sharp intellect. She began, "At the subatomic level, everything is interconnected. Particles, separated by vast distances, seem to 'communicate' with each other instantly, defying the limits of speed. This phenomenon is called 'quantum entanglement'."

Dr Aryan, ever the jester, quipped, "Ah, so it's like when my grandma knows I'm in trouble, even when she's miles away?"

The room erupted in laughter, but Dr Naina, undeterred, smiled and continued. "Exactly! It's the science behind intuition, perhaps."

Anika jumped in, her excitement palpable, "This is so similar to the ancient concept of '*Aakashic Records*', where all knowledge, past, present, and future, is stored in the cosmic realm. Seers and sages could tap into this information, transcending time and space."

Sharvil, playing the devil's advocate, remarked with a smirk, "So, you're saying our ancestors were the OG quantum physicists?"

Dr Aryan, laughing, responded, "Well, they didn't have fancy labs, but they certainly had deep insights!"

The discussions went on, drawing parallels between wave-particle duality and the dual nature of deities, superposition, and possibilities, and the collapse of wave function with focused intention in rituals and meditations.

One memorable session involved a debate on the nature of reality. Dr Naina proposed, "Quantum physics suggests that reality isn't objective. An observer affects the observed."

Anika, enthusiastically, responded, "This aligns with the *'Dristi-Srishti Vada'* from ancient scriptures, which suggests that the universe exists as we perceive it. Our perception shapes our reality."

Sharvil, trying to lighten the deep conversation, remarked, "So, if I close my eyes and believe hard enough, can I turn my coffee into a pizza?"

Dr Aryan, laughing heartily, retorted, "Only if you believe in the Pizza Particle, my boy!"

In the evening, as the sun set, painting the museum in golden hues, Anika and Sharvil sat in Dr Aryan's office, reflecting on the journey so far.

Sharvil, looking thoughtful, admitted, "You know, I started this journey as a sceptic. I wanted concrete proof, equations, and logic. But now, I've come to realize that sometimes, wisdom doesn't need validation. It just needs understanding."

Anika, her eyes shining, responded, "And sometimes, that understanding comes from looking at the old with new eyes, and the new with old wisdom."

In the aftermath of their enlightening discussions, Dr Aryan proposed a public presentation followed by a question and answer session. "The world needs to hear this. Merging the ancient and the modern can revolutionize how we perceive the universe," he declared.

Sharvil immediately agreed. "It's a fantastic idea, but public speaking? It's right up there with quantum physics in terms of complexity for me!"

Anika chuckled, "Come on! We've been through meditation misadventures, snowball fights, and even debated quantum mechanics with scholars. A public presentation should be a piece of cake!"

"Or a piece of pie," Sharvil replied with a smirk, making a sly nod to the mathematical constant pi, "because circles, and infinity, and... never mind."

The team set a date, booked a hall, and began preparations. They decided to split the presentation into three parts: Sharvil would handle the science, Anika the ancient scriptures, and Dr Aryan would bridge the gaps, sprinkling in his unique humour.

Their rehearsals weren't just about refining their content but also about synchronising their rhythm.

The day of the presentation arrived. The hall was packed, buzzing with anticipation. The lights dimmed, and a spotlight focused on the stage. Anika, looking elegant as always, took the audience through the wisdom of ancient scriptures. The audience was entranced as she narrated tales of cosmic dances, interconnected universes, and the power of perception.

Sharvil, using his drawings and small models, amazed the crowd next. He mixed funny jokes with clever ideas. "You know when your socks vanish in the laundry? Well, maybe they're in two places at once, like in a magic trick!" he said, making everyone laugh. He was comparing the mystery of disappearing socks to something called 'quantum superposition.' That's like when things can be in more than one spot at the same time, kind of like a magic trick.

Dr Aryan, bridging the gaps, was natural. His anecdotes, metaphors, and witty humour made the complex seem simple. "Quantum mechanics and ancient scriptures are like the two sides of a coin. Different, yet part of the same entity," he eloquently concluded.

Post-presentation, the trio was surrounded by an enthusiastic audience, eager to discuss and learn more. Among the sea of praises, one comment from an elderly lady stood out. "Young man," she said to Sharvil, "I never understood my grandson when he talked about quantum stuff. But today, I feel I can have a conversation with him. Thank you!"

Doubts and Dilemmas

The team was on board. 'Doubts and Dilemmas: A Live Q & A' was scheduled. The event garnered massive interest, with registrations overflowing.

On the day, the trio took the stage. The format was simple: anyone could ask a question, and they'd answer, blending logic with light-heartedness.

The first question came from a physics student. "You talk about quantum entanglement mirroring cosmic connection in ancient scriptures. Isn't that a stretch?"

Sharvil smiled, "Great question! Think of it this way: if you had told someone a hundred years ago about Wi-Fi, they'd have laughed. Invisible waves carrying data? But today, it's a reality. Similarly, ancient scriptures spoke of interconnectedness, just like entangled particles. Maybe our ancestors intuited what we're now discovering or yet to discover."

The next query was for Anika. "You spoke about the dance of Shiva mirroring the dance of subatomic particles. Isn't that oversimplifying?"

Anika replied, "The dance of Shiva, or Tandava, signifies the cosmic cycles of creation and destruction. It's a metaphor. Now, particles pop in and out of existence. So, while it's metaphorical, there's a poetic parallel. And sometimes, poetry captures truths that raw data can't."

A reporter asked Sharvil about the scientific base of all such discussions.

Sharvil replied, "Well, let me tell you about CERN (European Council for Nuclear Research). It's a remarkable place, located near Geneva, Switzerland, and it's one of the world's leading centres for scientific research, particularly in the field of particle physics. At CERN, scientists study the fundamental particles and forces that make up the universe, using the world's most powerful particle accelerator, the Large Hadron Collider, or LHC for short.

"Now, you might have heard about the Shiva statue outside of CERN. That statue was actually a gift from India, and it represents the close ties between India and CERN, which date all the way back to the 1960s and are still going strong today. In Hinduism, Lord Shiva is known for performing the Nataraj dance, which symbolizes Shakti, or the life force. The Indian government chose this deity as a symbol because they saw a metaphorical connection between Shiva's cosmic dance and the modern study of the 'cosmic dance' of subatomic particles at CERN. You see, India is one of CERN's associate member states, and CERN itself is a very diverse organization, with scientists coming from over 100 countries and 680 institutions. Even though so many countries are members still they have placed Natraj Statue there. May I take it as an explanation for your question," Sharvil said with a smile.

The reporter lay silent but was also smiling.

A man, visibly in his late fifties, stood up. "Dr Aryan, I've seen your humorous takes on serious matters. But don't you think there's a risk of trivialising knowledge?"

Dr Aryan, in his characteristic style, answered, "Sir, have you ever used humour to explain a complex idea to a child? It's the sugar that makes the medicine go down. We respect knowledge, and we respect that it needs to be accessible."

That man again asked, "How can you link love which is just an emotional state with something like quantum physics which basically deals with matter?"

Everyone started looking at Dr Aryan... it looked like Anika and Sharvil's findings were going to come to a huge halt. Dr Aryan took up the question, "Today, I want to share with you a perspective that might initially seem far removed from our everyday experiences but is deeply intertwined with the essence of our most cherished human emotions. I'm going to talk about love—not just any love, but that profound, often inexplicable connection that seems to defy distance and logic, much like the mysterious quantum phenomena that scientists are still trying to fully grasp."

"Imagine for a moment, the world of quantum physics—a realm where particles exist in multiple states at once, where actions performed on one particle can instantaneously affect another, no matter the distance between them. This is not the stuff of science fiction, but the reality of quantum entanglement and superposition. Now, think about the last time you felt a deep connection with someone you love. Isn't there a bit of that same mystery, that same defiance of the ordinary rules?

"Let's start with quantum entanglement. In the quantum realm, entangled particles remain connected so that the state of one (no matter how far away) instantly influences the state of the other. If we think of love in this context, we see a powerful metaphor for how deeply our lives are intertwined with those we care about. Just as the measurement of one particle affects the other, the joy, pain, or growth of one person can deeply affect their partner, no matter if they are together or apart. This bond speaks to a level of empathy and understanding that transcends the physical—a connection that many of us aspire to reach in our relationships.

"Now, let's consider the principle of superposition, where particles can exist in multiple states at once until they are observed. Isn't our own emotional state often just as complex and multifaceted? We are not merely happy or sad; we are a blend of many emotions and potentials, influenced by the people around us and the love we share. In love, we see that our partners, friends, or family members do not exist to us in a single state; they are multifaceted and whole, with an emotional spectrum that is rich and varied.

"The observer effect in quantum mechanics tells us that the mere act of observing can alter the state of a system. Similarly, the way we see the people we love can change them; our perception and our actions towards them can help them become the best version of themselves. This is the essence of nurturing love, the kind that sees the potential in the other and helps that potential come alive.

"Quantum tunnelling presents perhaps one of the most magical ideas—that particles can pass through barriers deemed impenetrable. How often does love show us that very same lesson? That the human spirit, fuelled by love and compassion, can overcome obstacles that seem insurmountable. A mother's love for her child is a perfect example of this. It knows no bounds. It reaches out, even in moments of immense challenge and difficulty, to support and uplift.

"These concepts from quantum physics offer us beautiful, if unexpected, parallels to the ways we experience and interact through love. But why talk about love in terms of quantum mechanics? Because it allows us to appreciate the profound, often inexplicable connections we share. It invites us to think deeply about the relationships that sustain and enrich our lives, pushing us to consider the unseen forces that bind us, not just physically but emotionally and spiritually.

"In our daily lives, this perspective urges us to cherish and nurture the connections we have. It encourages us to be observant and mindful of our actions and their effects on those we love. It challenges us to be agents of positive change, to be observers who bring out the best in others, and to believe in the power of love to transcend the barriers before us.

"As we ponder these ideas, let us not be daunted by the complexity of quantum theories, but inspired by their metaphorical resonance with our deepest human experiences. Let us take comfort in the knowledge that even in the face of life's many uncertainties and trials, the bonds we form are as profound as the most fundamental forces of the universe."

The questions kept coming. Some genuine, others sceptical, and a few downright hilarious. But with every question, the trio's responses were patient, understanding, and peppered with humour. They didn't shy away from admitting when they didn't have an answer, promising to delve deeper.

Sharvil concluded, "In closing, I invite each of you to reflect on the relationships in your lives. Think about the invisible threads that connect you to those you love. How can you strengthen those bonds? How can you foster deeper understanding and empathy? Just as the quantum world surprises us with its defiance of intuition, let our relationships be places of continual discovery and growth."

The trio united in their mission and bond, realized that with every doubt they cleared, they not only enlightened others but also deepened their understanding. They were not just seekers of truth; they had become its torchbearers.

The Talk

Anika, Sharvil, and Dr Aryan further went ahead to present their findings in a talk titled '*Mystical Physics: Ancient Meets Modern*'. The stage was adorned with two life-sized images: on one side was the iconic atomic symbol, and on the other, the swirling dance of Shiva.

The audience was a mix of intellectuals, students, journalists, and enthusiasts. A gentle murmur filled the hall as the lights dimmed.

Dr Aryan stepped onto the stage, his eyes gleaming. "Good evening, ladies and gentlemen. Tonight, we will take you on a journey, one that transcends time, beliefs, and maybe, just maybe, your own understanding."

Anika took over, "Imagine a world where the ancients understood more than they let on, where poetry met particles, and dance mirrored dimensions."

Sharvil, with a mischievous smile, remarked, "And you know, meditation could be like the original Wi-Fi, linking us to the whole universe. Maybe it's through what they call the Sahasrara chakra. Sahasrara is just a fancy Sanskrit word for the Crown chakra, which they say has a thousand petals. This energy centre is all about our connection to something bigger, like the spirit world, and it's where we find wisdom, a sense of being part of everything, and knowing ourselves better."

The audience chuckled. The tone was set.

Dr Aryan began with the basics of quantum physics, blending in humour. "Now, quantum mechanics is not just a great party topic to sound smart. It's the study of the teeny-tiny things that make up... well, everything. And sometimes, these particles behave like rebellious teenagers; unpredictable and full of surprises."

Anika took a poetic route, quoting from the ancient scriptures, "There's a verse that says: 'Everything is interconnected; everything is one.' Doesn't that sound a lot like the entangled particles of quantum mechanics?"

The audience leaned in, drawn to the parallelism.

Sharvil, with a playful tone, added, "And if you think about it, hasn't your mom's ability to know exactly what you're up to, no matter where you are, always felt a bit like quantum entanglement?"

This earned a hearty laugh from the audience.

Dr Aryan delved deeper into the realm of subatomic particles, making complex theories accessible with analogies and anecdotes. "If atoms were a family, electrons would be the toddlers. They're everywhere and nowhere at once!"

As the discussion transitioned from particles to waves, from certainties to probabilities, a beautiful dance began to emerge between the trio.

Sharvil shared an ancient mural of Aditya and Lasya from a cave, lovers separated by fate but connected by a force greater than any known to mankind. The tale mirrored the duo's journey.

Anika, her voice softer, added, "Aditya and Lasya were bound not by chains but by choice, by love. And isn't love the greatest force, one that even physics is yet to decipher?"

The atmosphere grew thick with emotion. And then, looking directly at Anika, Sharvil confessed, "Throughout this journey, amidst ancient verses and quantum quirks, I found another force, one that's inexplicable, undeniable. Anika, with every atom of my being, every waveform of my soul, I have realized that I am in love with you."

The hall was silent, then erupted in applause. Anika, her eyes glistening, replied, "Sharvil, in this universe of probabilities, the certainty of my feelings for you is the one thing I don't need quantum physics to explain."

Dr Aryan, clearing his throat dramatically, joked, "I always knew quantum mechanics had romantic potential. But didn't expect to witness it first-hand!" Everyone burst into laughing.

As they delved back into the academic, the audience was thoroughly engaged, hanging onto every word, every joke, and every revelation.

Sharvil concluded, "Maybe the ancients knew something profound, and perhaps, we're just beginning to grasp it. The dance of particles, the rhythm of the universe, the connections we forge; it's all intertwined."

Dr Aryan added, "Science doesn't subtract from the beauty and mystery of the universe. It adds to it."

Anika, holding Sharvil's hand, whispered, "And amidst this vast cosmos, the heart still finds its way."

The talk ended with a standing ovation. It had everything – depth, humour, love, and the eternal dance of the universe. People left with more than just knowledge; they left with a feeling of interconnectedness, a feeling of being a part of something much larger than themselves.

Eternal Love's Echo

On a moonlit night, Anika and Sharvil found themselves on the terrace of Anika's apartment building. The vastness of the night sky above them painted a serene backdrop, the city's hustle a distant hum.

Sharvil's fingers strummed a gentle tune on his guitar. Anika, resting her head on his shoulder, murmured "You know, their story has always been a part of our shared journey. Sometimes, I feel like their souls are guiding us, drawing parallels between their eternal bond and what we're building together."

Sharvil softly strummed a melodious tune, the notes reflecting Anika's sentiments. "Aditya and Lasya's bond spanned lifetimes. It is still present in murals and manuscripts. They were torn apart by circumstances but bound by love. Even in the face of challenges, they found their way back to each other, just like... well, us. Maybe they are still present in some universe."

Anika smiled, "Remember the reunion at that conference? Our paths crossed after so many years. I spilt coffee on your research notes, and instead of being angry, you made a joke about it being a 'quantum accident'. It felt like fate."

Sharvil laughed, "And when you started talking about ancient scriptures in a room full of quantum physicists, I was captivated. It was as if Lasya's wisdom was speaking through you."

"You know," Anika began, choosing her words, "Aditya and Lasya's love was rooted in understanding and sacrifice. They navigated societal norms, differing beliefs, and even the weight of history. But they had this unspoken connection, a pull towards one another. Do you ever feel that with us?"

Sharvil gazed deep into Anika's eyes. "Every time. Every moment we've spent deciphering ancient scriptures, exploring the Himalayas, and even the light-hearted banter with Dr Aryan, I've felt that connection."

"But you know," Sharvil continued, his tone turning serious, "even amidst all our humorous misadventures, I've always felt a deep respect for our bond. The way Aditya revered Lasya, honoured her knowledge and wisdom, I see and feel the same for you."

Anika's eyes shimmered with unshed tears. "And Lasya's unwavering faith in Aditya, her belief that love transcends boundaries, time, and space – I have that faith in us, Sharvil."

They sat there, wrapped in a shared blanket and each other, the stars their only witnesses. The stories of Aditya and Lasya echoed in their conversations, their laughter, and their silent moments.

Anika nodded, "And like them, we'll echo in eternity, won't we?"

Sharvil tightened his grip around her. "Always," he promised. "Always."

Quantum Quips

The next evening, in Anika's cosy apartment, Sharvil, stretching his arms, glanced over at Anika, who was engrossed in her evening ritual of sketching.

"Trying to capture the sunset again?" he teased, playfully peeking over her shoulder.

She laughed, nudging him away. Both came to the balcony.

The digital clock in Sharvil's apartment blinked at 7.00 p.m., signalling the start of their 'Saturday Night Quantum Night' – a tradition they'd started since their return. It was a playful and humorous attempt to discuss quantum mechanics and debunk myths, all while having fun.

That night, they'd invited a small group: friends, fellow academics, and some students passionate about quantum mechanics. The room buzzed with chatter as everyone settled in, waiting for the duo's comedic take on complex quantum concepts.

Anika took centre stage, a makeshift one using Sharvil's rug. "Ladies and gentlemen," she began dramatically, "Have you ever wondered why your lost socks never reappear? Well, it's all thanks to the world of quantum mechanics!"

The audience laughed, and Sharvil joined her, wearing mismatched socks, "Behold, the mystery of the quantum socks!"

Anika raised an eyebrow, "Shouldn't you be discussing Schrödinger's cat instead?"

Sharvil grinned, "Why talk about a cat in a box when we can discuss socks in a washing machine? Maybe they're both present and absent until we check?"

A ripple of laughter spread across the room. Their natural chemistry and comedic timing made even the most complex ideas approachable.

A student raised her hand, "Dr Anika, Dr Sharvil, what about quantum entanglement? Is that why when I can't find one earring, the other's gone too?"

Anika chuckled, "Ah, quantum entanglement! It's when two particles become interconnected, and the state of one instantly affects the other, no matter the distance. But earrings? I'd say that's more the mystery of the 'Quantum Handbag Abyss'."

Sharvil interjected, "Or perhaps a mini black hole in your jewellery box?" The room erupted in laughter.

A fellow professor asked, "What about the double-slit experiment? Can you explain that, humorously?"

Sharvil thought for a moment, "Imagine you're trying to sneak snacks into a movie theatre. If you've watched (or observed), you act like a good, law-abiding citizen. But unobserved? You're suddenly in two places at once, enjoying your forbidden snacks!"

Anika added, "But the moment the movie usher shines a light on you, you're back to being just one snack-less person, caught red-handed!"

A friend, trying to join the fun, asked, "What's your funny take on the uncertainty principle?"

Anika grinned, "It's like trying to find out if Sharvil finished the last cookie. The more precisely you try to figure out where he is, the less certain you are about how fast he's running away!"

Sharvil, mock offended, retorted, "Or, it's like trying to figure out Anika's tea preferences. The more you know about how much sugar she likes, the less you understand her tea's temperature preference."

"The jumble of vibrations or energy across multiple universes might explain why some folks experience déjà vu or feel like they remember bits from a past life."

As the evening progressed, they continued their humorous takes, from quantum superposition to particle-wave duality.

Quantum mechanics, often seen as a heady, challenging topic, was transformed into a series of light-hearted jokes and anecdotes.

As the night wound down, a student approached them. "You know, before this, I always found quantum mechanics intimidating. But you've made it relatable, and fun. Thank you."

Sharvil smiled, "That's the goal. To find joy and humour in learning. The universe is a vast, fascinating place. Why not have a little fun while exploring it?"

Anika added, "And if you ever figure out the quantum mystery of the missing socks, let us know!"

They all laughed during the night's conversations echoing the duo's ethos – that science and humour could coexist, making the journey of discovery a delightful and enriching experience for all.

Chapter 5
Unity

Collaboration and Comedy

The sun beamed down as Anika and Sharvil walked towards Dr Aryan's esteemed quantum physics lab, both visibly excited. As they pushed open the door, they were greeted by an unusual sight – Dr Aryan, in a lab coat, juggling beakers.

"Ah! Welcome, welcome!" Dr Aryan exclaimed, catching the last beaker just in time, and setting it down gently. "I find that juggling is the perfect warm-up for the mind. Now, come along. I've prepared a few experiments that are as entertaining as they are enlightening."

In the heart of the lab stood an apparatus that looked like an oversized hamster wheel. Dr Aryan explained, "This, dear friends, is the Quantum Wheel of Fate. We're testing the uncertainty principle but with a twist!"

Sharvil smirked, "So, instead of electrons, we're using... hamsters?"

Dr Aryan laughed heartily. "No, no. I need a volunteer!" Before they knew it, Sharvil was inside the wheel, looking quite uncertain himself.

As Dr Aryan started the machine, he said, "Now, Sharvil will run, and with each step, a series of lights will attempt to predict his speed and position. If the lights turn green, they're sure. If they turn red, well, they're as confused as we are!"

The room echoed with laughter as Sharvil tried to outwit the lights, speeding up and slowing down erratically. The experiment was a playful way to demonstrate Heisenberg's uncertainty principle. While Sharvil was slightly out of breath by the end, the experience left them all in splits.

Anika's turn came up next. Dr Aryan guided her to a table cluttered with about a dozen glasses, each holding different amounts of water and shaped uniquely. "Welcome to the Quantum Symphony," he declared with a flourish. "Each glass has its own special frequency. Your task, Anika, is to find the linked pairs!"

Anika looked puzzled. "Linked glasses?"

Dr Aryan nodded enthusiastically. "With a tap of your finger," he explained, "you'll make one glass ring. Another glass on the table will respond with a vibration, although you won't hear it. Your job is to use this gadget," he said, presenting a quirky device with antennas, "to find its matched pair!"

And so, the game began. Anika tapped each glass in turn, listening closely for the faint response from its paired partner. With each tap, she moved the detector closer, its beeps growing louder and more frequent as she approached the matching glass. Though the game seemed straightforward, it offered a tangible and enjoyable demonstration of how quantum entanglement and resonance work.

"Let me explain how this game illustrates quantum entanglement and resonance," began Dr Aryan, gesturing towards the array of glasses on the table.

"Each glass represents a quantum system. When Anika taps one glass, it sets off a chain reaction. Despite not being physically connected, another glass on the table vibrates in response. This somewhat mirrors the concept of quantum entanglement, where the properties of one particle become linked with the properties of another, regardless of distance."

He paused, allowing the significance to sink in before continuing. "Now, what you're witnessing is resonance. Resonance occurs when a system vibrates at its natural frequency in response to an external force. In this case, tapping a glass serves as the external force, causing it to vibrate at its natural frequency. And here's the fascinating part: the paired glass, which shares the same resonant frequency, responds in kind. It's like two dancers moving in perfect harmony, even though they're not physically connected. This tangible demonstration beautifully illustrates how objects can interact and synchronize through resonance, just like entangled quantum particles."

Hours flew by as the trio delved into one humorous experiment after another. From the 'Particle or Wave Relay Race' to the 'Schrödinger's Box of Surprises,' where they'd guess whether an object inside was intact or broken without opening it.

Sharvil, looking thoughtful, responded, "You know, Dr Aryan, today reminded me of why I fell in love with science in the first place. It's not just about formulas and theories; it's about curiosity, wonder, and the joy of understanding."

Anika nodded in agreement. "Collaborating with you has been an eye-opener. Your humour-infused approach makes these complex concepts come alive."

Dr Aryan smiled warmly. "Ah, young ones. Science is as much about the heart as it is about the mind."

As they left the lab that evening, their steps light and hearts full, Anika and Sharvil realized that the day's adventures were more than just experiments. They were a celebration of the joyous dance between science and humour, and the unforgettable memories they'd carry forever.

Love's Resilience

The day had transformed into a soft dusk, with shades of orange and pink painting the sky. Anika and Sharvil sat on a wooden bench, overlooking the tranquil Powai lake, the water reflecting the myriad hues of the setting sun.

Anika leaned back, looking at the horizon. A gentle breeze played with Anika's hair as she began, "They first met at a village fair. Lasya was dancing, her feet barely touching the ground, her spirit free. Aditya was a wandering musician, and the moment he saw her, he started playing a tune, one that mirrored her dance steps perfectly."

"They didn't need words," Sharvil mused, "Their souls communicated through dance and music and ultimately through vibration and energy."

Sharvil's voice had a touch of sadness, "But life wasn't always kind to them, was it?"

Anika sighed, "No, it wasn't. But they say that every evening, the villagers would gather around them, and in the gentle melodies of Aditya's flute and the graceful movements of Lasya's fingers, they'd find solace, hope, and love."

The silence that followed was filled with reverence for a love that had withstood the test of time and adversity. Sharvil squeezed Anika's hand, "Their story... it makes you believe in the kind of love that transcends lifetimes."

Anika smiled, leaning her head on Sharvil's shoulder, "It's a reminder that love isn't just about the joyful moments, but about standing strong, hand in hand, even when the storms of life threaten to pull you apart."

As night deepened and stars twinkled above, Anika and Sharvil sat there, their hearts filled with the tales of the past, but also with dreams and hopes for their own future. They began reading the scroll.

And so, the journey began,
In the heart of the silent void,
Stars twinkle, and galaxies whirl,
Stories of old, mysteries untold,
In the vast cosmic swirl.
Moons that wax and wane in grace,
Planets with rings and fiery faces,
Every atom, every space,
Is a testament to nature's embrace.
Black holes, with their might,
Swallowing everything, even light,
Yet, in this infinite night,
Hope twinkles, ever so bright.
Blue and green, a sight to behold,
Earth, with tales of brave and bold,
Mountains high, oceans cold,
A beauty, never growing old.
Stardust beings, that's what we are,
Born from a supernova, from afar,
In our veins, flows cosmic tar,
Destined to dream, to raise the bar.

Anika sighed, "Poetry has the power to bridge the gap between the complexities of science and the simplicities of human emotion." Sharvil nodded in affirmation.

Eternal Echoes

Hours flew by as Anika and Sharvil dove deep into their scroll, every so often encountering hilarious mismatches. At one point, Anika held up a verse that talked about the 'fire of the soul'. After a lot of deliberation and debate, they decided it was possibly talking about the body's metabolism. Or maybe passion? Or perhaps it was just a poetic way to describe heartburn!

Sharvil leaned on the railing beside her. “It’s funny you say that. I’ve been having similar thoughts. In quantum physics, we talk about particles being in a superposition, existing in multiple states until observed. What if love is the same?”

Anika turned to him, her eyes searching his. “Do you think we, in our essence, are eternal too? That beyond this life, our consciousness, our essence, our love... continues?”

Sharvil took a deep breath, feeling the weight of the question. “From the moment we’re born until we leave this world, there’s a sense of ‘me’ inside each of us. It’s always there, like a constant observer of everything going on around us. This feeling never fades; it’s like a timeless part of who we are. Even in Vedic thinking, they say that the idea of us being separate from the world is just a trick of the mind famously known as the illusion of separation. In reality, we’re all connected to each other and everything in the universe. It’s like we’re all pieces of a big puzzle, fitting together to make one big picture.

Sometimes, when two people meet, they feel a special bond, like they’re somehow connected to each other from a shared source. This feeling is called true love. Sadly, it’s becoming harder to find these days because many folks are too focused on money and casual dating. “I’ve always believed that there’s more to us than our physical selves. If energy can’t be destroyed, why should consciousness? Our body might be temporary, but the essence of who we are, the love we feel... I think it’s timeless. Just like the love story of Aditya and Lasya.”

She took a sip of her tea, letting the warmth seep into her. “It’s a comforting thought, isn’t it? That love is eternal.”

Chapter 6
The Unfathomable Find

Guarded Secrets

There is a Sanskrit saying

> **यथा पिण्डे तथा ब्रह्माण्डे, यथा ब्रह्माण्डे तथा पिण्डे।**
>
> As is the individual, so is the universe, as is the universe, so is the individual.

The next morning, Anika and Sharvil awoke to find themselves standing at the majestic entrance of an ancient library. But this wasn't just any library—it was to house texts and scriptures older than recorded history itself. The sheer size of the library was overwhelming, with tens of thousands of books meticulously organized on countless shelves stretching across hundreds of narrow aisles. It seemed like a treasure trove of knowledge, holding a vast collection of books, manuscripts, and documents. It looked like while students were allowed to peruse and borrow most titles, access to the Restricted Section was tightly controlled, requiring access through specific Sling Rings adorned with Sanskrit symbols for entry.

As they approached, an old man with a silver beard and kind, piercing eyes beckoned them forward. He wore robes with intricate patterns that seemed to move and shimmer, almost as if they were alive. His attire was simple and humble, reflecting his ascetic lifestyle and detachment from worldly possessions. He had a serene and noble appearance, expressing wisdom and compassion His demeanour radiated strength, grace, and devotion, embodying the ideal of a divine sage in Hindu mythology.

"Welcome, seekers," he greeted them with a deep, resonant voice.

Anika, always curious, inquired, "Are you the librarian here?"

"Wait, a minute... aren't you the same old man we met behind the tree?" Anika asked with a puzzled expression.

The Librarian smiled warmly and replied, "You can call me Tanzin, the librarian, the caretaker, the saint of the Himalayas, or the monk who greeted you at the monastery – it's your choice. By the way, my name is Kalanabha. My duty is to assist those who seek knowledge."

The old man chuckled softly. "Some call me as the Keeper. But most know us as the Guardians of the Vedas."

Sharvil stepped forward, offering the invitation they had received. "We were summoned here, though we're uncertain of the reason."

Kalanabha gestured for them to enter. "You are worthy. This is not a place from your world, it is an entirely different realm. Only those deemed worthy are summoned here. You have come close to unravelling the very existence itself. You have been called to aid you on your quest. Come, let's walk and talk."

As they walked through the aisles, Kalanabha began, "The Vedas are not just texts; they're the embodiment of knowledge, timeless and universal. And while many interpret their verses in myriad ways, few understand their true depth."

Anika whispered, leaning closer to Sharvil, "It's like being in a living dream. These books... they breathe."

Sharvil nodded, equally mesmerized. "But why are we here?"

Kalanabha led them to a secluded corner, where a pedestal stood, holding an ancient book having the all-seeing owl and an infinity loop image on its cover.

"The Vedas have always spoken of the universe's truths. But there are verses... mantras, if you will, that hint at not just this universe but many. The Multiversal Mantras."

Anika's heart raced. "Are you saying the Vedas knew of other universes?"

Kalanabha nodded. "Infinite universes, each with its own cosmic rhythm. And while many are similar, they're not identical. The Mantras are keys to understanding and travel through them."

"When we speak, we're not just making noise. Every sound creates a form, and there's a whole science behind using sounds in a specific way to create the right kind of form. Different sounds activate different energies in our body. But if we just repeat sounds without understanding, it can make our minds dull. However, if we're aware and understand what we're saying, it can be powerful. That's where mantras come in. Each mantra activates a specific energy in our body. Some are for spiritual growth, called 'Siddhi,' while others are for material progress, known as 'Vruddhi.' And just like that, there are mantras to help us understand the concept of the multiverse, we have a fancy name of it for you: The multiverse manta."

Kalanabha turned to Sharvil with a knowing look. "Do you doubt my words? Ask Anika. She had a glimpse of that at the monastery herself."

Sharvil glanced at Anika, his expression filled with questions. Anika affirmed with a nod. "It's true. I saw it, but I didn't mention it to anyone because I thought no one would believe me."

Sharvil's disappointment was evident. "You could have told

me. We're in this together, remember?" Anika's eyes softened. "From now on, I promise to share everything with you."

Sharvil, sceptical but intrigued, turned to Kalanabha and inquired about the Book, "And how do you propose we decipher them? These texts have been studied for ages."

With a mischievous twinkle in his eye, Kalanabha responded, "Ah, young man, that's where modern science and ancient wisdom merge. You both are uniquely positioned to do so. Anika, with her understanding of the ancient scripts, and Sharvil, with his knowledge of science."

A soft laugh escaped Anika. "Sounds like a plot from a science fiction novel."

Kalanabha chuckled. "Ah, dear child, the universe has a sense of humour more vibrant than any fiction you can conjure."

As they talked, shadows lengthened, and the library grew dimmer, but the scroll on the pedestal seemed to glow with an inner light.

"The Mantras won't be easy to decipher. And there are those who'd prefer their secrets remain hidden," Kalanabha warned, his tone turning serious.

Anika's determination flared. "Knowledge should be free, not hoarded."

Kalanabha smiled warmly, placing a gentle hand on her shoulder. "You cannot teach a toddler the intricacies of the doctorate degree course. You have to be worthy of it."

Kalanabha emphasized the importance of the Book, cautioning Sharvil and Anika, "This book holds great power, but remember, it must be used with the right intention. If you seek to use it solely for personal gain, it will find its way back here, for good. However, if your intent is pure and aimed at benefiting others, the book will remain with you, guiding your path."

Sharvil asked, "So, intent is the key?"

Kalanabha replied, "Exactly."

As the duo left the library, the weight of their new responsibility heavy on their minds, Sharvil squeezed Anika's hand. "Together?"

She smiled, "Always. Now across every universe."

Beyond the Books

The morning sun poured through the window of Sharvil's study, illuminating stacks of manuscripts, the Book, and an assortment of hi-tech gadgets. On the wall hung a large whiteboard, scribbled over with equations, drawings, and, oddly enough, a doodle of a cat with glasses.

A poster of a quote by famous Psychologist Carl Jung, "In all chaos, there is a cosmos, in all disorder a secret order."

Anika walked in, holding two cups of steaming chai. "Progress report, Mr Scientist?"

Sharvil, his hair ruffled and glasses askew, looked up, slightly startled. "Anika! Just the interruption – uh, I mean inspiration I needed." He attempted to clear a space on his desk, pushing aside a mound of books, only to have a stack of papers topple over.

Anika chuckled. "Your organisational skills never cease to amaze me."

Sharvil smirked, taking the chai from her. "But that's where you're wrong. This is all... strategically placed chaos."

As Anika took a seat across from him, she glanced at the whiteboard. "Is that... a cat?"

Sharvil blushed slightly. "That's Schrödinger's cat. I thought, considering we're delving into quantum physics, he deserved a place."

And what about the quote?

"This quote by Carl Jung means that even in situations that seem chaotic or disordered, there is often a hidden pattern or structure. It suggests that there is an underlying order or harmony in the universe, even when things appear random or confusing."

Anika grinned, "Of course, how silly of me. So, decoded the universe yet?"

Sharvil sighed. "It's... challenging. Some of these texts seem straightforward. Like, 'the universe sings in harmony.' Okay, that might refer to resonant frequencies. But then there's stuff like 'The lotus blooms in cosmic mud.' What does that even mean? Is the universe the lotus or the mud? Or both?"

Anika tried to stifle her laughter. "You're overthinking it."

Sharvil raised an eyebrow. "Am I? Look at this." He opened the Book to a page with a beautifully painted lotus. "This might be talking about cosmic birth from chaos, or it could be a gardening tip!"

Anika giggled, "Maybe it's about finding beauty in complexity?"

Sharvil mockingly gasped, "You mean, I need to turn gardener to understand the universe?"

She winked, "It couldn't hurt."

They both burst into laughter.

After a moment, Anika, her eyes scanning the texts, said, "You know, we have to feel these texts, not just read them. They're not just words; they're experiences and emotions. Maybe it's not about decoding but understanding. Describing experiences like the multiverse or meditation is like trying to explain what sweetness or sourness feels like. Just as we can't fully capture the taste of sweetness or sourness in words, we also can't completely express the feeling of these experiences. They're beyond words and can only be understood through symbols or metaphors."

Sharvil looked thoughtful. "So, instead of being the scientist, we should be thinking like a poet?"

She smiled warmly. "Or perhaps, a bit of both?"

He took a deep breath, glancing at the texts with newfound appreciation. "Alright, let's start again. Together."

As they delved back into the Book, it was evident that the journey wouldn't be just about unravelling ancient secrets but also about understanding each other and finding the balance between logic and emotion, science, and sentiment.

Throughout the day, Sharvil would occasionally burst into fits of laughter upon encountering particularly cryptic verses, while Anika would often counter with profound interpretations that seemed to emerge straight from the heart.

That evening, as the sun cast golden hues across the room, the duo sat back, exhausted yet exhilarated.

Sharvil mused, "Maybe it's not about finding exact answers but rather embracing the questions, the mysteries."

Anika nodded, "And perhaps realizing that some things, like love, are beyond mere words and equations i.e., can't be defined in terms of objective science."

He smirked, "Speaking of love, how about some dinner? My treat for the wisdom you brought to today's chaos."

She chuckled, "Only if it's as cosmic as the texts."

"Deal," he said with a grin, "but no guarantees about the mud."

Dreams and Dimensions

The sun had long set in her apartment. Anika's mind buzzed with the secrets she'd uncovered from the ancient Book she'd been studying. Little did she know that the night would be anything but ordinary.

Anika, exhausted from hours of reading, lay down and slowly drifted into sleep. As the line between wakefulness and dreams began to blur, she felt a gentle pull, as if some invisible force was reeling her in.

Anika whispered as she drifted, "What's happening? Where am I going?"

Suddenly, the room around her dissolved, replaced by a vast expanse of blue and gold, a celestial skyline that defied all logic. She was floating, surrounded by countless stars, each flickering and pulsating to a rhythm, a universal heartbeat.

Below her, Anika saw a world similar yet distinct from Earth. Towering mountains made of shimmering crystals, rivers that flowed mid-air, forests glowing with iridescent light. And amidst this otherworldly scenery, she spotted a figure that seemed oddly familiar.

"Anika?! Is that... is that really you?" the familiar voice called out.

"Sharvil? How are we here, in this dream? Or is this some cosmic prank?"

"I honestly have no clue, but it's brilliant, isn't it? Like an artist's fantasy, only real."

The two took a moment to marvel at the beauty around them, trying to make sense of this shared dreamscape. As they floated hand in hand, they came across an ethereal tree, its roots and branches intertwined in intricate patterns, pulsating with energy.

"Do you feel that, Sharvil? The tree... it's calling out to us."

"I knew those esoteric texts had some deep stuff, but this is beyond my wildest imagination!" he replied, chuckling.

They approached the tree, and as they touched it, memories and emotions flooded into them, not just from their past, but from countless lifetimes, from countless universes. They witnessed love stories that transcended time, space, and reality.

Anika was teary-eyed. "It's Aditya and Lasya. Their love is... it's everywhere, in every universe. Our love is just a reflection of theirs."

"It's eternal. Just like theirs. Just like this tree. It's all connected."

As dawn approached, the dream started to fade. The ethereal world, the tree, the emotions, all began to blur.

Anika cried frantically, "Sharvil, I don't want to lose this. I don't want to forget!"

Sharvil said, "We won't. We'll find our way back. Together."

The luminous world vanished, and Anika jolted awake in her bed. The room was drenched in the soft hues of dawn. She immediately grabbed her phone.

Anika called Sharvil, "Sharvil! Did you...?"

Sharvil replied, "Every single moment. It was real."

Anika smiled, a tear started rolling down her cheek, her heart filled with wonder, love, and infinite possibilities. The journey had just begun.

A Deeper Dive

The next day in Anika's apartment, the sunlight streamed through the windows of the room, casting golden patterns on the wooden floor. Anika sat cross-legged, surrounded by piles of old manuscripts and the Book, her attention on one particular page containing an intricate Sanskrit mantra. Sharvil lounged on a nearby sofa, a digital translator in hand, looking both intrigued and befuddled.

"This mantra, Sharvil... it's not just words. It's sort of an encoded key."

Sharvil said with a mock-serious tone, "Well, I tried chanting it this morning, and neither did I levitate nor did a portal to another dimension open. Perhaps it's broken?"

Anika laughed, "It's not a magic spell! It's like a complex equation in quantum physics. We need to understand and unlock its potential."

Sharvil said, “Okay, Professor Anika, the enlightened soul.”

After many attempts, Anika and Sharvil found themselves facing disappointment each time. They experimented with different locations: the balcony, the roof, under a tree, and even trying various yoga poses. Yet, nothing seemed to work. Then, like a bolt from the blue, Sharvil recalled Kalanabha’s words about being omnipresent to aid everyone. Anika, intrigued, asked how they could reach out to him. They decided to close their eyes and silently call upon him, but their efforts were in vain.

Hours passed, and suddenly the doorbell chimed. An elderly postman stood there, seeking addresses for two partial letters. Anika noticed each letter contained only half an address. Quick to decipher the mystery, she suggested combining both halves to form a complete address, which happened to be nearby. The postman smiled mysteriously and responded, “exactly” before departing, leaving Anika and Sharvil pondering over his words.

Undeterred by their previous failures, they again attempted various methods: reciting mantras, lighting candles, and invoking different rituals. However, their endeavours yielded no results. Anika, struck by a sudden thought questioned the significance of the postman’s word “exactly.” Could he be Kalanabha? Sharvil with a spark in his eyes proposed that they should recite together while holding hands, drawing inspiration from the unified souls of Aditya and Lasya in their shared story. They embarked on this new approach, hoping for a breakthrough.

As they chanted the mantra together, holding hands, a palpable energy surrounded them. The room seemed to hum with a mysterious force, and a shimmering aura enveloped them.

Sharvil exclaimed, visibly excited, “Anika, did you feel that? It’s like the air itself is alive!”

Anika nodded, “Yes, I felt it too. It’s like the wisdom of the ancients is speaking to us through these vibrations.”

Sharvil grinned, "So, what's our next move? Decoding ancient mysteries or becoming seers ourselves?"

Anika chuckled, "Why not both? But first, let's experiment."

They ventured to different places to chant the mantra, eager to explore its effects. In the forest, the trees swayed gently in harmony with their chanting. By Powai lake, ripples formed on the water's surface, echoing the rhythm of their mantra.

Sharvil observed, "Nature seems to dance to our words. It's like we're in tune with the universe."

Anika added, "I believe this mantra might be the key to unlocking doorways to other realms, like the ones we saw in our shared dream."

Sharvil nodded, "It's a bold theory, but after everything we've experienced, it's worth exploring."

As Anika and Sharvil finished their discussion, they noticed Gita, an older woman looking to have deep knowledge, watching them quietly. Approaching them, Gita spoke gently, "You two are exploring ancient wisdom with youthful curiosity. But do you really understand the power of the mantra you're chanting?"

Anika, showing respect, said, "We're trying to, ma'am. The mantra's meaning is still unclear to us, and we're seeking guidance to understand it better."

Gita smiled, "Exploring ancient wisdom is a journey that needs patience and humility. The mantra holds the essence of the cosmos, a power beyond the ordinary. But remember, with great knowledge comes great responsibility."

Sharvil, intrigued, asked, "Does that mean we could cause trouble if we don't understand it properly?"

Gita replied thoughtfully, "Not exactly trouble, but the energy in the mantra is strong. It should be used with care and understanding, or it could have unintended effects."

Guided by Gita's wisdom, they searched for answers about the universe and themselves. They learned to approach their studies with an open mind, realizing that true wisdom is about asking questions. They found joy in learning and marvelled at the wonders of the universe.

Together, they explored their own minds and learned to use their thoughts wisely. They knew their journey would be hard, but they faced it bravely, knowing they had the wisdom of the ages to guide them.

In the end, Anika and Sharvil discerned that true wisdom is not just about knowing things but also about understanding and respecting the mysteries of life. They knew their journey was far from over and looked forward to uncovering more secrets of the universe together. They needed Gita's help. They decided to go to Powai lake again where they found Gita.

Gita took them under her wing, guiding them in understanding the mantra's deeper meanings. They learned to not only recite it but to embody its essence. With practice, they could harness its energy and even use it for healing.

Sharvil remarked after a session, "This feels like a soul workout, exhilarating yet draining."

Anika agreed, "It's demanding, but the results are profound. This mantra isn't just a tool; it's a source of wisdom and protection."

Gita added, "Remember, it's not just about power; it's about love and unity. The universe reflects your innermost self."

One evening by the lake, bathed in the sun's golden glow, Anika and Sharvil shared a moment of revelation.

Anika reflected, "Our love is intertwined with the universe's harmony. Each time we chant, we reaffirm our eternal bond."

Sharvil teased, "So, we're the ultimate power couple of the cosmos?"

Anika laughed, "Perhaps! But more importantly, our love resonates with the timeless truths embedded in these mantras."

As they chanted together, the universe seemed to echo in agreement, the mantra not just a set of words, but a testament to love, unity, and the infinite connections that bind everything together.

Hesitations

In their shared practices, Anika and Sharvil often stumbled upon remarkable discoveries. One day, as they delved into their chanting, a nearby tree seemed to shiver, its leaves rustling with otherworldly energy. For a fleeting moment, the tree appeared ghostly, revealing a glimpse of another realm.

Anika's voice trembled with awe, "Sharvil, did you...?"

"Yes," he interrupted, his tone tinged with alarm, "What if our actions disrupt another universe? This is beyond us."

Feeling the weight of their newfound power, they sought the counsel of Gita, the elder known for her wisdom. Hoping for guidance, they approached her with their concerns.

Gita, ever composed and insightful, remarked, "Every power has the potential to create and destroy. It is the intention behind its use that determines its course. Understand your actions and the ripples they may create in the fabric of existence."

That night, as they sought solace in the warmth of their shared space, Anika experienced a vivid dream. Universes unfolded before her, each with its own unique tapestry of serenity and chaos. Startled awake, she found comfort in Sharvil's embrace.

"Sharvil," she whispered, her voice tinged with fear, "I'm scared." Drawing her close, he murmured soothingly, "So am I."

Later, they engaged in deep contemplation. Anika's voice rang with earnestness, "This isn't just about us anymore. Our actions have consequences that ripple across dimensions. Are we truly prepared for what lies ahead?"

Sharvil took a moment to collect his thoughts before responding, "Perhaps we need to acquire more wisdom before venturing further into the unknown."

Their mentor, Gita, observed their growth with pride, her eyes sparkling with wisdom. "The mantras you explore may be ancient, but their teachings are timeless. Young souls, tread cautiously, for the path you walk holds the potential to shape the destinies of many."

Anika held onto Sharvil, her heart overflowing with emotion. "Through all the uncertainty and challenges, there remains one constant – us."

He smiled tenderly, his gaze meeting hers with unwavering affection. "Our souls are intertwined in a journey unlike any other, bound together for eternity."

As they continued to explore the mysteries of the universe, they encountered both triumphs and setbacks. Each experience, whether joyful or challenging, brought them closer together, strengthening their connection and reaffirming their commitment to their shared path.

Despite their growing knowledge and understanding, there were moments of doubt and fear. The enormity of their quest weighed heavily on their shoulders, and they often found themselves questioning their own abilities and the impact of their actions.

Yet, through it all, they remained steadfast in their determination to unlock the secrets of the cosmos and harness the power of the ancient mantras for the greater good. With Gita's guidance and their unwavering bond, they faced each obstacle with courage and resilience, knowing that together, they were capable of achieving anything.

As they delved deeper into the meanings of the mantras, they discovered hidden truths and unlocked ancient wisdom that had been lost to time. With each revelation, they grew more attuned to the rhythms of the universe and the interconnectedness of all things.

Their journey was not without its challenges, but with each challenge came growth and enlightenment. They learned to embrace the unknown and trust in the guidance of their hearts, knowing that their love and determination would see them through even the darkest of times.

In the end, it was their unwavering faith in each other and their shared vision that led them to unlock the true power of the mantras. Together, they embarked on a journey that would change the course of their lives and the fate of the cosmos itself, forever bound by their love and their quest for knowledge.

Eternal Threads

Anika's visions often transported her to realms beyond the ordinary, offering fleeting glimpses into the tapestry of history and the interwoven threads of fate. Among the myriad images that danced through her mind, one constant theme emerged – the timeless love story of Aditya and Lasya. Theirs was a love that transcended time and space, echoing through the corridors of eternity.

One afternoon, as Anika and Sharvil sought shade under the ancient peepal tree that stood sentinel outside their home, she was overcome by a sudden wave of déjà vu. Closing her eyes, she was enveloped in a kaleidoscope of memories: Aditya, a valiant warrior in one realm, a gentle poet in another, and a revered sage in yet another, with Lasya, his forever companion, by his side in every incarnation. Across countless dimensions, their love remained unchanged, an unbreakable bond that defied the boundaries of existence.

Observing Anika's trance-like state, Sharvil whispered softly, "What do you see?"

Anika took a moment to gather her thoughts, her voice tinged with awe. "Aditya and Lasya, they're everywhere, Sharvil. Their souls traverse the vast expanse of the cosmos, bound together by an unyielding love that knows no bounds. It's... it's breathtaking."

That evening, they sought the counsel of Gita, the venerable sage whose wisdom was as vast as the universe itself. In the flickering light of the oil lamps that adorned Gita's humble abode, they shared Anika's vision, each word imbued with a sense of wonder and reverence.

Gita, her weathered hands deftly stirring a fragrant concoction, listened intently before offering her insight. "The love of Aditya and Lasya is legendary," she began her voice a gentle melody that filled the room. "Their souls are intertwined, destined to find each other across the vast tapestry of existence. In each life, in each realm, they are drawn together by the magnetic pull of their love."

Sharvil, ever the sceptic, arched an eyebrow in curiosity. "Always? Isn't that a bit far-fetched?"

Gita chuckled softly, her laughter a soothing balm to their restless souls. "Love, my dear boy, is the most potent force in the universe. It transcends time and space, weaving its way through the fabric of reality. Aditya and Lasya's love is a testament to the enduring power of the human heart."

Anika, lost in thought, pondered aloud, "If such love exists, why do we not see more of it in our own realm?"

Gita leaned forward, her eyes sparkling with ancient wisdom. "Love, my child, is not always loud and ostentatious. It exists in the quiet moments, the stolen glances, the tender gestures. Aditya and Lasya's love may be rare, but traces of it can be found in every corner of the universe, including within your own hearts."

Sharvil cast a meaningful glance at Anika, his gaze softening with understanding. "Do you think...?" he began, his voice trailing off.

Anika met his gaze, her eyes alight with possibility. "We could be them, in some small way. Bound by destiny, connected by love."

Sharvil, always one to approach things with a practical mindset, found himself unexpectedly drawn to the ancient mantras. Anika unveiled a parchment inscribed with the sacred chants they were to practice. With a mix of curiosity and determination, they embarked on their journey to master the mantras.

As they began their practice, Sharvil attempted to mimic the solemn tone and tempo he had heard from Gita. However, his initial efforts fell short, producing sounds more akin to a frog's croak than a sacred chant. Anika couldn't suppress her laughter, and when it was her turn, her rendition was more towards a Bollywood melody than a solemn invocation.

Realizing their need for guidance, they sought out Gita. Patiently, Gita explained the essence and origin of each syllable, emphasizing the importance of understanding and feeling rather than mere pronunciation.

With Gita's support, Sharvil slowly began to master the intricacies of the chants. Anika, equally determined, poured her focus into refining her pronunciation. Their home echoed with comical reaction to the mantras with each attempt punctuated by laughter.

But with perseverance and Gita's unwavering guidance, they began to find their rhythm. The chants, once stumbling blocks, now flowed with increasing ease and grace.

One evening, bathed in the golden glow of the setting sun, Anika and Sharvil sat side by side, their voices merging in harmonious unison. As the vibrations of their chants filled the room, they felt a profound connection not only with each other but with the very fabric of the universe itself.

Opening their eyes, they shared a moment of understanding and accomplishment. Their journey, once fraught with uncertainty and doubt, had brought them closer together than ever before. With each attempt, they grew in skill and confidence, paving the way for new discoveries and deeper insights into the mysteries of the multiverse.

Their practice sessions slowly became a ritual, a shared space where they could explore the depths of their own capabilities and the boundless wonders of the universe. Each evening, they would gather in their humble abode, surrounded by flickering candlelight and the soft strains of the mantras.

Over time, they noticed subtle shifts in their own beings. Sharvil, who was once commited to his reliance on logic, began to embrace the more intuitive aspects of the mantras. Anika, who was always attuned to her emotions, found a newfound sense of groundedness and clarity in her practice.

Their bond, too, blossomed in ways they had never imagined. Through the laughter and the frustration, the moments of triumph and the setbacks, they forged a connection that transcended the mundane concerns of everyday life.

As they delved deeper into the mysteries of the mantras, they discovered hidden layers of meaning and symbolism. Each syllable seemed to hold within it a universe of possibilities, a doorway to realms beyond their wildest dreams.

But perhaps the greatest lesson they learned was the power of perseverance and dedication. In a world filled with distractions and uncertainties, their commitment to their practice became a beacon of light, guiding them through even the darkest of times.

And so, as they continued on their journey, Anika and Sharvil knew that they were not alone. With the wisdom of the ancient mantras as their guide and the unwavering support of each other, they were ready to face whatever challenges lay ahead, confident in the knowledge that their bond was stronger than any obstacle they might encounter.

First Glimpse

The days had begun to blend seamlessly as Sharvil and Anika delved deeper into their mantra practices. Despite the initial hiccups, their dedication had started to produce a certain resonance in their surroundings. It was during one of these sessions, as dusk painted the sky in hues of amber and purple, that they first felt it – a tangible shift, subtle but unmistakable.

Their cosy living room, usually filled with the scent of burning incense and the soft glow of candlelight, suddenly grew colder. The candles flickered wildly as if responding to a sudden gust, though the windows were securely shut.

Anika, sensitive and attuned to energies, sensed it first. Her voice lost its tempo, her chanting ceased, and her eyes flew open to meet Sharvil's equally puzzled gaze. "Did you feel that?" she whispered, her voice barely audible over the growing hum in the room.

Sharvil nodded, struggling to find words. "It's like... a vibration, a ripple."

Before they could further ponder the sensation, their surroundings began to transform. The walls of their living room stretched and morphed, displaying images much like a movie projector. They saw vast landscapes, unfamiliar yet eerily beautiful – mountains that floated, rivers that flowed upside down, and cities made of crystals.

"What is happening?" Anika murmured, clutching Sharvil's arm, her eyes wide with awe and a tinge of fear.

Sharvil, equally amazed but always the protector, pulled Anika close. "It's the multiverse," he whispered. "We're getting a glimpse."

The images changed, shifting rapidly from one universe to another. They saw beings – some human-like, others completely alien, living their lives, laughing, loving, and facing challenges not too different from their own.

And then, amidst the whirlpool of images, they saw a familiar pair – a couple that looked strikingly like Aditya and Lasya, but in different avatars, in different dimensions. They were dancing in one universe, warriors in another, and scholars in yet another.

Sharvil and Anika watched, mesmerized. It was a proof to the eternal nature of love, to the countless forms and lives it took, and to the countless universes it permeated.

As suddenly as it began, the echo ceased. The images vanished, the walls returned to their normal state, and the room's warmth enveloped them once more. The candles, which had been flickering madly, stabilized.

Both sat in silence for a long moment, processing the enormity of what they had just witnessed.

Finally, Anika spoke, her voice trembling with emotion. "Sharvil... that was... breathtaking. But why? Why did we see it?"

Sharvil, deep in thought, responded, "The mantras, our intent, our connection to Aditya and Lasya all converged. We tapped into something ancient and powerful."

The revelation that the profound experience Anika and Sharvil had when they witnessed the glimpses of different universes and the eternal dance of Aditya and Lasya in various forms. This experience shook them to their core, as they realized the vastness of the multiverse and the timeless nature of love that permeates through it. It was a moment of profound insight and understanding, where they felt the interconnectedness of all existence and the power of love as a unifying force.

The couple, still overwhelmed by the revelations, held onto each other, feeling the pulse of every universe, every dimension. In that moment, they realized that love, in all its forms, was the true bridge between worlds.

Decision to Dive

The morning light filtered through the curtains, painting the room in hues of gold. Sharvil and Anika sat facing each other, a heavy silence hanging between them. The events of the previous night weighed on their minds, urging them to confront their newfound revelation.

Anika broke the silence, her tone resolute. "What we saw wasn't random, Sharvil. Those glimpses into other dimensions felt like messages, maybe even calls for help."

Sharvil met her gaze, acknowledging her insight. "So, you think we should take action?"

She nodded firmly. "Yes. We've been entrusted with this knowledge for a reason. It's not enough to just witness; we have to intervene."

"But how?" Sharvil's practicality kicked in. "The multiverse is vast, overwhelming. Where do we even start?"

Anika smiled, a glimmer of determination in her eyes. "Remember our project? Combining ancient wisdom with modern science? We already have the tools – the mantras, our intent, our connection. Maybe it's time to put them to use."

Sharvil chuckled. "You mean become guardians of love across dimensions?"

She nudged him playfully. "Why not? Imagine ensuring every love story finds its happy ending, no matter the universe."

Sharvil pondered her words. "It does sound beautiful, but are we equipped for this? We're dealing with powers we barely understand."

Anika reached out, placing her hand over his. "Love may be mysterious, but it's also the strongest force in the universe. If we can make a difference in even one story, wouldn't it be worth it?"

He grinned. "You always did have a way of making the impossible seem possible."

She smirked. "Someone has to balance out your overthinking."

They shared a moment of laughter, the tension easing between them.

Then, Sharvil grew serious. "Okay, let's say we're in. How do we start?"

Anika paused, deep in thought. "We need to delve deeper into the multiversal mantras and the Book and understand them better. And we trust in our intent, our love. The universe showed us those glimpses for a reason."

Sharvil agreed. "Right. But we can't do this alone. We'll need guidance."

She nodded. "The Guardians of the Veda, The Kalanabha. They might have answers. He hinted about the Multiversal Mantras for a reason."

Sharvil raised an eyebrow. "Another adventure, partner?"

Anika squeezed his hand. "Always, with you."

Together, they embarked on a journey to unravel the mysteries of the multiverse, armed with determination, love, and the belief that even the smallest actions could have profound consequences across dimensions.

Their first step was to deepen their understanding of the multiversal mantras. They spent hours poring over the Book, seeking hidden meanings and insights. With each revelation, their confidence grew, and they began to grasp the intricacies of the cosmic language.

As they perused deeper, they realized that the key lay not just in reciting the mantras but in understanding their underlying principles. The mantras were more than mere words; they were gateways to different realms, bridges between worlds.

Their studies led them to the Guardians of the Veda, the revered keepers of ancient knowledge. With excitement, they sought an audience with the Kalanabha, hoping to gain his wisdom and guidance. With pure intent, they called Kalanabha and suddenly they heard a knock on the door. Anika opened the door with smile.

Their meeting with the Kalanabha was unlike anything they had imagined. The sage greeted them with warmth and kindness, his eyes twinkling with ancient wisdom. He listened intently as they recounted their experiences and aspirations, nodding thoughtfully at their words.

When they finished, the Kalanabha spoke, his voice resonating with power and authority. "You have been chosen for a great task, young ones. The multiverse is vast and unfathomable, but love is the thread that binds it all together. With your pure hearts and steadfast determination, you have the power to make a difference."

He imparted to them the knowledge of the Multiversal Mantras, ancient incantations that transcended time and space. He told them that their purpose is to understand love and to help others comprehend it as well. Feeling the need of the moment, Anika requested Kalanabha to be present in all realms to guide them. Kalanabha smiled and graciously promised to fulfill her request. With his guidance, they began to unlock the true potential of the mantras, tapping into their hidden energies and vibrations.

Armed with this newfound knowledge, Sharvil and Anika set out on their mission to safeguard love across dimensions.

Universe Unveiled

Sharvil stood at the centre of the room, the Book spread open before him. Meanwhile, Anika was engrossed in setting up a circle of aromatic herbs and rare crystals, creating an ambience that blended ancient practices with modern understanding. As they prepared for what lay ahead, a sense of uncertainty lingered in the air.

Anika glanced up, meeting Sharvil's eyes. "Are you sure about this?"

Sharvil swallowed hard, his usual confidence tinged with vulnerability. "Not entirely. But if we don't try, we'll never know."

She offered him a reassuring smile. "Remember, the key is intent. Let our intent guide us."

He chuckled nervously. "How could I forget? Our love's pretty much got us into this multiverse mess."

She playfully threw a petal at him. "Oh, hush! Always with the humour, even at times like this."

Sharvil winked. "Helps with the nerves."

Taking their positions opposite each other within the circle, they both inhaled deeply, savouring the intoxicating aroma of the herbs. They began to chant the mantra in unison, their voices rising and falling in a beautiful, rhythmic cadence.

As minutes passed, a subtle energy began to stir. The room seemed to vibrate, the air thickening, and the temperature dropping. The crystals in the circle began to glow, their colours vibrant and pulsating.

Suddenly, Anika felt a strong tug, a pull from deep within. It wasn't just physical; it was emotional, spiritual even. She glanced at Sharvil, whose eyes were wide with wonder. Without needing to speak, they both understood they were on the brink of something monumental.

With a final combined push of intent and emotion, the world around them seemed to stretch, distort, and then snap back into focus. But it was different.

Everything suddenly calmed down.

They found themselves atop a floating island, surrounded by ethereal trees with luminescent leaves. The sky above was a shade of lilac with two moons gracing the horizon. Below, more islands floated like dandelions in the wind, each with its unique topography.

Sharvil looked around in awe. "Well, that's not our usual morning view."

Anika, still processing the shift, whispered, "We did it. We're in another realm."

They explored this new world, marvelling at the similarities and differences. They discovered a civilization somewhat akin to theirs but advanced in harmony with nature. There were no vehicles or machines; instead, the inhabitants rode on magnificent winged creatures, and their homes were seamlessly integrated into the towering trees.

Upon interacting with the locals, they learned of a love story that had caused ripples in this world, not unlike that of Aditya and Lasya. Two souls, perpetually searching for each other but always just out of reach due to a curse.

Anika's heart went out to them. "We need to help them."

Sharvil nodded. "That's why we're here."

However, their visit did not go unnoticed. The guardians of this realm, ethereal beings of light approached them, their presence powerful yet gentle.

"Why have you come here?" one of them asked, his voice echoing like a soft melody.

Anika stepped forward, her voice firm but respectful. "To understand a love story. To feel that love knows no bounds, not even those of different universes."

The being seemed to study them, its form shimmering. "Your intent is pure. Proceed with caution. The fabric of our realms is delicate."

Kalanabha smiled and whispered softly, "I told you Intent is the key."

Sharvil gave a small bow. "Thank you. We'll remember."

And thus, their adventure in this new realm began. Their shared purpose, to celebrate love and its eternal power, drove them forward. With every leap, with every chant, they uncovered the vast tapestry of existence, one where love was the ever-persistent thread.

Together, they navigated through challenges, learning and growing with each step. Their journey was not without its trials, but their unwavering determination and pure intent guided them through even the darkest moments.

As they ventured deeper into this realm, they discovered the interconnectedness of all things, the delicate balance that held the universe together. And through it all, their bond only grew stronger, a beacon of light amidst the vast expanse of the multiverse.

In the end, it wasn't just about unravelling mysteries or overcoming obstacles; it was about embracing the journey, with all its twists and turns, and finding beauty and meaning in every moment. And as they continued on their path, they knew that their love, their intent, would always guide them home.

Chapter 7
The Cosmic Portal

In the cluttered study, surrounded by the Book and ancient relics, Anika, and Sharvil, stood before an intricately carved wooden table that bore the mysterious palm leaf manuscript. The room was humming with a palpable tension as they prepared to recite the last verse of Multiversal Mantras which Kalanabha had entrusted to them. But this time they were backed by their newfound knowledge and experience.

"Are you sure about this?" Anika's voice quivered slightly, a mix of excitement and fear as she glanced at Sharvil, who was studying the manuscript with a furrowed brow.

Sharvil looked up, his eyes meeting hers with a reassuring confidence. "It's what we've been preparing for, isn't it? If Kalanabha believes we can handle this, then we can. Besides, think of what we might discover."

Holding hands tightly, Anika and Sharvil started chanting the ancient mantras together. As they repeated the verses, their voices built a powerful rhythm that seemed to pulse through the air. Soon, the entire room vibrated, as if their chanting was actually changing the space around them. The walls began to blur and fade, and before they knew it, they were no longer in their small study but were floating in a vast, open cosmos.

As Anika and Sharvil floated through the cosmos, they were surrounded by breathtaking celestial phenomena. Spiral galaxies stretched out before them like giant whirlpools, spinning gracefully in the vastness of space. These galaxies, with their arms delicately wrapped in stardust, seemed to perform a slow dance of gravity and light.

Nearby, the smoother, more serene glow of elliptical galaxies added a calming contrast to the dynamic universe. They seemed like tranquil islands in the vast ocean of space, each one a silent guardian of countless stars.

Deeper into their journey, they encountered clusters of stars that sparkled like celestial gems. Tight-knit groups of stars, bound together by gravity, shone brilliantly against the dark backdrop of the universe. Among these, one cluster, which they playfully named 'Luminous Embrace,' appeared particularly vibrant, its stars mingling in a bright, tangled dance.

The journey brought them next to a nebula they named 'Painter's Haze,' a vast cloud of gas and dust alive with the birth of new stars. Its swirls of vibrant colours painted a picture of cosmic creation, each hue telling a story of heat, light, and elemental fusion.

Close by, 'Twin Sparkles,' two closely situated star clusters, caught their attention. These clusters, dense with stars, seemed almost merged into one dazzling collection, reflecting each other's light and magnifying their brilliance.

Another remarkable sight was the 'Celestial Bell,' a planetary nebula shaped like a delicate bell, its edges glowing in hues of red and blue. This ethereal structure, a remnant of a star like our sun, radiated with the beauty of its past life, offering a glimpse into the fate of all starry beings.

Surrounding these stellar phenomena were clouds that twisted and turned, creating a mesmerizing visual spectacle. The universe seemed to be at work painting itself, using the palette of light and the canvas of the void.

This cosmic voyage was more than a travel through space; it felt like a timeless journey through the very life cycles of stars and the natural artistry of the universe. Each new view brought awe and wonder, reminding Anika and Sharvil of the vast, intricate web of existence that connected them to the farthest reaches of the universe.

Overwhelmed by the scale and beauty of their surroundings, they felt a profound connection not just to each other, but to the cosmos itself. It was a powerful reminder of their small yet significant place in the grand tapestry of the universe, participants in a boundless dance of celestial bodies.

As their chanting tapered off, the cosmic ocean calmed, and a path formed beneath them. It looked as if it were woven from the stardust itself, shimmering with energy and leading them forward. At the end of this stardust path, an impressive arena emerged, glowing with soft celestial light, giving the impression of a grand amphitheatre suspended in the cosmos.

The arena where Anika and Sharvil stood seemed to float in the void of space, a breathtaking amphitheatre surrounded by the infinite expanse of the cosmos. The platform they were on shimmered under their feet, as if stardust had been woven into its very essence, reflecting the light of distant stars and nebulae.

Above them, the sky was not a sky at all, but a vast canvas displaying the cosmic ballet of galaxies and celestial phenomena. The edges of the arena were marked by arches that glowed softly, their light gentle and inviting, casting long, ethereal shadows across the ground. These arches seemed to pulse with a life of their own, rhythmically glowing in sync with the distant hum of the universe—a cosmic pulse that resonated with the energy around them.

The central area, directly beneath the cosmic light show, was illuminated by a cluster of light that seemed both ancient and alive, spotlighting the figures of Aditya and Lasya. The light did not blaze; rather, it bathed them in a luminance that seemed to lift the very essence of their beings, highlighting their faces and the traditional celestial garments they wore. Each thread of their attire sparkled as if sewn with fragments of light, their clothes billowing slightly as if caught in a silent cosmic wind.

Surrounding the central stage was a semi-circle of tiered steps that appeared to be carved from the same crystalline material as the platform. Each step seemed to be a slice of the night sky itself, dotted with tiny lights that mimicked the stars. These steps served as seats for the assembly of luminous beings who had come to witness the ceremony, each being radiating a serene light that contributed to the overall luminescence of the arena.

The air itself in the arena was alive with a gentle vibration, a subtle echo of the mantras that had been chanted. It felt as though the very atmosphere was charged with anticipation, waiting for the momentous vows to be exchanged at the centre of this celestial gathering.

This arena, set against the backdrop of the infinite universe, provided a stage not just for a ceremony but for the celebration of a bond that transcended time and space, witnessed by the cosmos itself. Anika and Sharvil watched, mesmerized by the ceremony. The priest's words, though spoken in an unknown language, felt strangely familiar, tugging at something deep within their souls.

"Do you feel that?" Anika asked, her voice barely a whisper. "It's as if we've known these words, this ceremony, in another life."

Before Sharvil could respond, a serene voice spoke from behind them. Turning, they saw Kalanabha, his form shimmering with a subtle light. "What you witness is the eternal union of Aditya and Lasya, a ceremony transcending time itself. This is not just a spectacle, but a reflection of your own destinies intertwined with theirs."

"How is this possible?" Sharvil asked, struggling to grasp the surreal reality.

Kalanabha smiled, his eyes gleaming with wisdom. "The multiversal mantras you recited are keys to unlocking the layers of existence. Aditya and Lasya's story is a mirror of your own. You, Sharvil and Anika, are their echoes across time, brought here to witness this union to understand the depth of your connection."

As the ceremony continued, Aditya turned to Lasya, speaking heartfelt vows that seemed to transcend the boundaries of space, promising eternal love, and fidelity. Lasya responded with equal passion, her voice imbued with a timeless love that seemed to envelop Anika and Sharvil, warming their hearts and soul.

Kalanabha continued, "Their vows are the belief and feeling that maintain the balance of the universe. Today, you are here to rekindle your bond that spans lifetimes, to remember and reaffirm your vows."

The revelation left Anika and Sharvil profoundly moved. Tears streamed down Anika's cheeks, not of sadness but of overwhelming joy and realization. Sharvil, ever the sceptic, found himself believing in the impossible, feeling an indescribable bond with Anika that he now understood was as old as time itself.

"Remember," Lasya spoke, her voice now a soft but clear whisper carried on a cosmic breeze, "love transcends the physical vessels of time and space. It is the ultimate truth, the core of all existence."

Aditya added, "And today, you have rekindled a flame that was perhaps dimmed but never extinguished. Carry this light back to your world. Let it guide you through the darkest nights and the stormiest days."

The gathering slowly began to dissipate, the entities fading into stardust, leaving Anika and Sharvil alone in the clearing. The cosmic portal that had brought them there winked once more before fading, signaling their return to their own dimension.

Anika turned to Sharvil, a tear tracing her cheek. "Whatever comes next," she said, her voice firm despite the tear, "we face it together, with the strength of the love we've seen today."

Sharvil pulled her close, his embrace a fortress against any storm they might face. "Together," he affirmed, "today, tomorrow, and across every universe we might encounter."

Their shared smile was a silent vow, a reflection of the eternal union they had witnessed, a promise not just made but destined.

As the celestial light began to fade and the stardust settled, Anika and Sharvil stood silently, still enveloped in the afterglow of the profound ceremony they had witnessed. Just as they were about to discuss their overwhelming feelings, a familiar figure materialized before them. It was Kalanabha, the wise old sage whose guidance had first set them on this incredible journey.

Kalanabha's eyes twinkled with ancient knowledge as he observed the couple, seeing their confusion and awe. "Anika, Sharvil," he began in a voice that seemed to echo with the wisdom of the ages, "what you have witnessed today is a revelation for the soul."

Anika, her voice trembling with emotion, asked, "Kalanabha, were we really... I mean, in our past lives, were we Aditya and Lasya? How is that possible?"

Sharvil, still trying to process the ceremony's implications, added, "Yes, and how could we possibly remember this now? It feels like a dream, yet so vivid and real."

Kalanabha nodded gently, a smile playing on his lips. "Indeed, you were once Aditya and Lasya. This cosmic ritual you witnessed was your own from eons ago, transcending time and space to reach you now when you most needed to see it."

He stepped closer, his presence comforting yet awe-inspiring. "In each life, souls seek each other out to complete unfinished business, to heal old wounds, and to grow together. Your souls have been intertwined through the cosmos, always seeking to find balance and harmony."

Anika looked at Sharvil, her hand reaching out to his, seeking reassurance. Sharvil, his scepticism fading into a new, unexplored acceptance, clasped her hand tightly.

"But why now, Kalanabha? Why show us this memory at this moment?" Anika asked, her voice a mix of curiosity and desperation.

"The universe works in mysterious ways," Kalanabha explained. "It senses when souls are ready to awaken to their past, to learn from it, and to use those lessons to influence their present and future. You both stand at a cliff, your spirits ready to ascend to a higher understanding of love and commitment."

Sharvil, his mind always seeking logical explanations, struggled with acceptance. "So, what you're saying is, our love in this life... it's not new? It's a continuation of something ancient, something cosmic?"

"Exactly, Sharvil," Kalanabha affirmed. "Your love is as old as the stars themselves. Each life brings challenges, separations, and reunions. This life is your opportunity to resolve what was left uncompleted, to heal what was once broken."

Anika felt a rush of memories flood through her, images of laughter, tears, separation, and joy with Sharvil—or Aditya, as she now remembered. She saw glimpses of their lives together, the pain of parting, and the joy of reunions. The emotions overwhelmed her, and tears streamed down her cheeks.

"And now, knowing this, what are we supposed to do?" she whispered, her voice heavy with the weight of countless lifetimes.

Kalanabha placed a comforting hand on each of their shoulders. "Live this life with love and purpose. Let the knowledge of your eternal bond guide you to make choices that bring joy and peace. Remember, every interaction, every decision creates ripples through the cosmos. You are not merely living for yourselves, but for the universe."

Sharvil, now visibly moved, nodded slowly. "It's a lot to take in, but if our love is truly this powerful, this eternal, then I want to honour it. Not just for us, but for the universe."

Anika squeezed Sharvil's hand, a newfound resolve shining in her eyes. "Let's make this life our best one yet, Sharvil. Let's heal, let's love, and let's help others find their way, just as we have found ours."

Kalanabha smiled, his task completed, his message delivered. "You have understood well. Go forth with my blessings, and remember, the universe always watches, always listens, and always guides."

With a final nod, Kalanabha faded into the ether, leaving Anika and Sharvil alone. Their hearts and souls forever changed. They knew now that they were not just traversing their life's path, but were guardians of a love that spanned the multiverse. As they turned to leave, a sense of purpose filled their steps. They were not just lovers in this life – they were soulmates in every sense of the word, destined to echo through eternity.

After the ethereal figure of Kalanabha dissolved into the shimmering cosmic backdrop, Anika, and Sharvil found themselves standing beneath the vast, star-filled sky, the silence around them thick with revelation and awe. They grasped each other's hands tightly, both comforted and intimidated by the profound truths they had just encountered.

Sharvil, ever the analytical mind, was the first to break the silence. "Anika, do you realize the gravity of what we've just learned? Our love is a continuum, something that's been ours over many lifetimes."

Anika nodded, "Yes, it feels like we've been given a glimpse into the universe's heart where our story is intertwining through the ages."

They sat down on the grass, still holding hands, needing the connection to ground them as they processed their experiences.

Kalanabha's words echoed in their minds: "This gift of remembrance is rare. Most souls drift through lifetimes, unaware of their past bonds. You have been chosen to remember because your love has the strength to transcend the usual boundaries that time and flesh impose."

Anika looked deep into Sharvil's eyes, seeking and offering reassurance. "He said we were chosen, Sharvil. That our love could help bend the universe towards harmony. How do we even begin to live up to that?"

Sharvil squeezed her hand, a gesture that spoke of support and shared strength. "We start by accepting this gift fully. We embrace our love, past and present, and let it guide us. Maybe it's about more than just us—maybe it's about how we interact with the world, how we share this love."

They spent the next few moments in silence, each lost in thoughts of lifetimes past, the weight of their cosmic journey pressing upon them. Finally, Anika spoke up, her voice soft but firm. "Kalanabha said our love transcends physical existence. That means it's more than just emotions—it's a force, a kind of energy that can affect the world around us."

"Yes," Sharvil mused, his scientific mind intrigued by the concept. "If we think of love as an energy, then it makes sense that it can influence things, change outcomes, maybe even heal. Our love could be a tool, a way to bring about the harmony Kalanabha spoke of."

The idea seemed to invigorate them, giving them a purpose beyond their personal happiness. "We should be mindful, then," Anika suggested. "Mindful of how we use this energy. We can start small, affect the people around us, spread kindness and understanding."

"And maybe," Sharvil added, "that's how we bend the universe towards harmony. Not with grand gestures, but with small, everyday actions powered by love."

Anika smiled, inspired by the notion. "Let's do it. Let's be those agents of harmony. Let's live our love out loud, in actions and in words."

Their conversation drifted towards planning how they could implement this new understanding into their daily lives. They discussed starting a community outreach programme, perhaps using their story to inspire others, to teach about the power of love and unity.

As the night deepened, they lay back, staring up at the cosmos that had just revealed so much to them. "It's a lot to take in," Sharvil said, his voice a mix of wonder and determination.

"But it's beautiful, isn't it?" Anika responded, her voice full of hope. "To think that our love is part of the cosmos, part of the universe's fabric."

"Yes, it's incredible. And terrifying. And absolutely beautiful," Sharvil agreed.

Return to reality

As the ethereal chords of the universe's melody slowly began to fade, Anika and Sharvil felt the tangible pull of their own world summoning them back. The cosmic portal through which they had witnessed the eternal union of Aditya and Lasya—their own past selves—began to swirl with a complex pattern of stars and nebulous clouds, signalling the end of their transcendent journey.

The air around them thickened, and the brilliant lights of the otherworldly dimension dimmed into the creeping familiarity of their own reality. Sharvil squeezed Anika's hand as they both braced for the return, their hearts heavy with the weight of newfound knowledge yet buoyant with the realisation of their eternal connection.

As the last strains of cosmic energy dissipated, they found themselves spinning through a vortex of colours and sounds. It was as if the fabric of reality itself was being stitched back together, thread by ethereal thread. The world around them twisted and turned in impossible ways, reminiscent of scenes Sharvil had seen in a Dr Strange movie, where dimensions folded upon themselves and landscapes bent in mind-bending patterns.

Suddenly, with a soft but firm jolt, they were back. The familiar walls of Anika's Mumbai apartment wrapped around them, grounding them in the mundane but comforting reality of home. They stood for a moment in silence, the only sound their synchronized breathing and the faint hum of the city life outside the window.

Anika looked around, her gaze lingering on the small details of her apartment—the stack of books on the coffee table, the draping of the curtains, the array of potted plants basking in the dim light filtering through the blinds. Everything looked the same, yet nothing felt the same anymore.

"Feels like we've been away for only a moment," Anika whispered, her voice echoing slightly in the quiet of the room.

"In a way, we have," Sharvil replied, his voice low, reflecting the profundity of their experience. "Or perhaps we've just lived another lifetime in a span of moments."

They moved closer to each other instinctively, seeking comfort in their shared presence. As they did, the room seemed to settle, the earlier distortions of their return fading into the tranquillity of normalcy. It was as though their apartment, with all its familiar quirks, was a solid anchor in the sea of their multiversal explorations.

Sharvil walked over to the window and pulled back the curtain slightly, peering out into the bustling streets below. The city was unchanged, unaware of the cosmic journeys undertaken by two of its inhabitants. The normalcy of the scene outside contrasted starkly with the profundity of their recent experiences.

Turning back to Anika, Sharvil reached for her hands, holding them in his as he looked into her eyes. "What now?" he asked, the magnitude of their journey hanging between them.

Anika smiled, a serene, knowing smile that seemed to light up the room. "Now, we live this life—the one we have here, together—with all the love and understanding of our past lives fuelling us. We share our story, help others find their paths, and maybe, just maybe, make a little more sense of this vast, beautiful universe."

"Let's go to SoBo," he suggested, his voice laced with excitement.

Anika looked puzzled for a moment. "SoBo? What's that?"

Sharvil smiled, enjoying the moment of mystery. "SoBo—it's short for Southern Bombay. It's one of the most vibrant parts of the city, and it includes Marine Drive, one of my favourite places."

Anika's face lit up with understanding and delight. "Oh, Marine Drive! Why didn't you just say that? Let's go. It sounds like a perfect evening plan."

As the sun dipped below the horizon, casting a golden glow over Mumbai, Anika, and Sharvil found themselves strolling along the picturesque Marine Drive. The promenade, affectionately known as the Queen's Necklace, was bathed in the warm light of street lamps that twinkled like stars against the twilight sky, mirroring the glittering Arabian Sea beside them.

The gentle breeze carried the salty tang of the sea, mingling with the buzz of the city as it wound down for the day. Marine Drive, with its graceful arc from Nariman Point to the jam-packed Girgaum Chowpatty, was alive with the sounds of laughter and the gentle lapping of waves. Families, couples, and solitary figures alike found solace along this scenic stretch, each absorbed in the serene beauty of the evening.

Anika held Sharvil's hand, her eyes reflecting the shimmering lights across the coastline. "It's beautiful, isn't it? How the lights curve along the shore, like a necklace laid down by some giant hand," she remarked, her voice tinged with awe.

Sharvil smiled, looking around at the vibrant scene. "It's beautiful... But being here with you, it feels like we're a part of this painting, this moment frozen in time."

They paused for a while at a spot where the view of the sea was particularly breathtaking. The sky had turned a deep indigo, but the city lights kept the darkness at bay, casting a magical glow that danced on the water's surface.

"Do you remember the first time we came here?" Sharvil asked, his gaze lingering on the horizon where the sea seemed to meet the sky.

Anika nodded, her smile widening. "How could I forget? You were trying so hard to impress me with your knowledge of the stars, pointing out constellations."

"And miserably failing," Sharvil added with a laugh. "I think I made up half of them. But you were impressed by my creativity, weren't you?"

"Maybe a little," Anika teased, leaning her head on his shoulder. "But I was more impressed with how real you were, how you turned every mistake into a moment of joy. That's when I knew..."

"That you were stuck with me," Sharvil finished for her, a playful twinkle in his eye. They both laughed, the sound mingling with the symphony of the waves and the distant hum of the city.

They resumed their walk, the comfortable silence between them speaking volumes. Every now and then, Sharvil would point out a particularly vibrant spot where the lights hit the water just right, creating a sparkling path that seemed to lead straight to the stars.

As they approached Girgaum Chowpatty, the aroma of street food filled the air, tempting them with promises of spicy chaat and sweet kulfi. But they were content to just be together, their steps synchronized, their hearts in tune with the rhythmic beat of Mumbai's night.

"It's moments like these," Anika said softly, "that remind me how much I love this city, and how much I love being here with you."

Sharvil pulled her close and kissed her. "And it's moments like these that remind me how infinite love can be, like this necklace, continuous and unbroken."

"Anika, have you ever considered how everything in life seems to follow certain patterns?" Sharvil began breaking the silence that had settled between them. "Birth, death, reincarnation, and even eternity—it's like the universe has set patterns that it repeats over and over."

Anika nodded, intrigued by where his thoughts were leading. "Yes, it's fascinating. It seems like there's a rhythm or a cycle to everything, not just in nature but in our lives, too."

"And if you think about it," Sharvil continued, "our journey, encountering our past lives, it wasn't random. It's like we were meant to see that, to remember. Maybe understanding these patterns can help us figure out a lot more about how things work—about life, love, and the universe itself."

"You might be onto something," Anika agreed, her mind racing with possibilities. "Maybe we should talk to Dr Aryan about this. He's spent years studying how ancient wisdom and modern science intersect. He might offer some clarity or even validate our experiences."

Sharvil nodded in agreement, grateful for her proactive approach. "That's a good idea. Let's meet with him tomorrow. I have a feeling he might shed some light on these patterns we're talking about."

The next day, Anika, and Sharvil made their way to Dr Aryan's office, a space filled with books, artifacts, and an air of quiet contemplation. Dr Aryan welcomed them warmly, intrigued by the urgency in their request for a meeting.

Once settled, Sharvil wasted no time in sharing their experiences. "Dr Aryan, we've been through something extraordinary. We encountered what we believe were our past lives and witnessed a union that transcended time and space. It has made us think about the patterns that the universe seems to follow."

Dr Aryan listened intently, his eyes reflecting a mix of fascination and understanding. When they finished, he leaned back in his chair, stroking his chin thoughtfully.

"Your experiences align with many ancient teachings," he began. "Many cultures believe in the cyclical patterns of life and the universe—what you've described about patterns, including reincarnation and eternal bonds, is deeply embedded in many philosophies and religions."

Anika, seeking further confirmation, asked, "Do you believe that the universe has these patterns? And what about love? Could it really be this powerful force that connects everything as we experienced?"

Dr Aryan smiled, a knowing glint in his eyes. "Yes, I do believe in the patterns of the universe. And as for love, it is indeed a powerful, connecting force. Modern physics and ancient metaphysical teachings both suggest that everything in the universe is interconnected. Your experience of love transcending time and dimensions is a beautiful, profound manifestation of this principle."

Dr Aryan leaned back in his chair, adjusting his glasses as he addressed Anika and Sharvil, who were sitting across from him in his cluttered office, filled with books and artifacts. Let me tell you something. "You know, there's something utterly fascinating about the Fibonacci sequence, or the Golden Ratio, as it's sometimes known," he began, his voice filled with a mix of enthusiasm and scholarly interest.

Anika leaned in, her curiosity piqued. "What about it?"

Dr Aryan spun his computer monitor towards them. "This pattern appears far more often in nature than one might expect, suggesting a kind of universal connectivity. Though it's not completely proven, the evidence is quite compelling."

He clicked through to an image of a sunflower's seed head. "Take a look at this," he continued, pointing to the screen. "The arrangement of seeds in sunflowers follows a Fibonacci pattern, optimized for maximum sun exposure. And it's not just in flora; this sequence can be seen in the structure of galaxies and even the patterns of hurricanes."

Sharvil raised an eyebrow. "In hurricanes, you say?"

"Yes, indeed," Dr Aryan affirmed, scrolling down to show more examples. "And there's more—consider the DNA molecule. It measures 34 angstroms by 21 angstroms for each full cycle of its double helix spiral. These numbers are Fibonacci numbers, suggesting that even at a microscopic level, there's a hidden order."

Anika nodded slowly, clearly fascinated. "So, it seems like the universe might follow specific patterns, even if we haven't completely proved it yet?"

"Exactly," Dr Aryan replied, his eyes twinkling behind his glasses. "And here's something that might interest you even more. The concept of this sequence was known way before Fibonacci in the West. An ancient Indian scholar named Pingala described similar patterns in his analysis of Sanskrit poetry, centuries before Fibonacci's time."

"That's remarkable," Anika responded, her interest deepening. "It really makes you wonder if everything in the universe is interconnected in ways we're only beginning to understand."

Dr Aryan chuckled, closing his laptop. "Precisely. It's as if the universe has its own language, and these patterns, these numbers, are part of it. Who knows what other secrets are waiting out there, hidden in plain sight?" While coming out of Dr Aryan's Lab, Anika held Sharvil's hand in hers. "Sharvil, do you remember the first time we met? Everything seemed so simple back then. I never imagined our path would lead us to uncover such incredible truths about ourselves and the universe."

Sharvil smiled, squeezing her hands gently, "I do remember, Anika. We were both so different back then. I was the sceptic, always questioning everything. And you, always curious, always open to the mysteries of the universe."

"It's strange," Anika continued, "how our journey to understand Aditya and Lasya's story led us back to our own. It feels like we've come full circle."

"Yes," Sharvil agreed, "but with each circle, we grow. We expand. Every turn on this spiral has taught us something profound about our love and our place in this cosmos. It's a circle, but it's also a spiral, moving upward, evolving."

Anika nodded thoughtfully. "It's like each chapter of our lives adds layers to our love and existence, making it stronger, more resilient. I want to continue this journey with you, Sharvil. Not just to live through our days, but to make each day count, to make our love a testament to the truths we've discovered."

"I feel the same," Sharvil confessed. "Before, I used to think of love as something that just 'is.' But now, I see it as something we do, something active. Our love is our strength, our power. It's what allows us to make a real difference."

They leaned forward, the candlelight casting their faces in a warm glow, and sealed their vows with a kiss that held the promise of enduring love and eternal commitment.

In that moment, Anika, and Sharvil felt a renewed sense of purpose. Their love, enriched by the cosmic truths they had embraced, was not just a private joy but a public declaration of their commitment to live meaningfully, making each action a reflection of the universal love they had witnessed and lived. As they planned, they were not just planning for two—they were planning for the universe, their love a bridge between the stars and the hearts of people everywhere.

In their cozy Mumbai apartment, Sharvil, and Anika sat facing each other, a small table cluttered with books about quantum physics, ancient Vedic philosophy, and journals filled with their notes lay between them. The room was humming with the soft music of sitar flowing from the speakers, blending the old with the new, much like their lives.

Sharvil, looking deeply into Anika's eyes, started the conversation that had been brewing in his mind. "Anika, do you remember the mantra Kalanabha gave us? The one about love weaving through the cosmos?"

Anika nodded, her face lighting up with the memory. "Yes, it was beautiful. It said something about love being the thread that connects the stars. It's a powerful idea."

"It is," Sharvil agreed, picking up a journal. "And I've been thinking about how we can live that truth. How do we make that mantra a real part of our everyday lives?"

Anika leaned in, intrigued. "We start by being that thread, Sharvil. We weave love into our actions, our words, and our thoughts. Every interaction is a chance to strengthen that cosmic fabric."

Sharvil smiled, inspired by her vision. "I love that. It's like every kind word, every genuine smile, and every act of kindness is us weaving love into the universe."

Anika reached across the table to hold his hand. "Exactly. And it's not just about big gestures. It's the small moments, too. The way we talk to the shopkeeper, the way we handle frustrations, even the way we think about ourselves."

Sharvil nodded thoughtfully. "It's about consistency, isn't it? Being mindful that every moment is an opportunity to contribute positively to the cosmic whole."

"Yes, and it's about gratitude as well," Anika added. "Gratitude opens us up to love. When we are thankful, we are more likely to act out of love, more likely to be patient, to be kind."

Sharvil picked up a pen and scribbled in the journal. "I'm going to make it a practice to start each day by listing things I'm grateful for. It could be as simple as a good cup of coffee or as deep as my gratitude for our journey and our love."

"That's wonderful," Anika beamed. "And what about incorporating it into our community? Maybe we could start a gratitude circle. A monthly meeting where people come together to share what they're grateful for, to spread love and positivity."

Sharvil loved the idea. "Let's do it. And let's not stop there. We could organize workshops that combine these teachings with practical exercises in mindfulness and gratitude."

As they talked, their ideas grew, forming a plan that felt both exciting and meaningful. They discussed reaching out to local schools to introduce programs that taught children about interconnectedness and kindness from a young age.

"Imagine if we could help instill these values early on," Anika mused, her eyes sparkling with enthusiasm. "We could help shape a more connected, more loving world."

"And we could use our story as an example," Sharvil suggested. "Not just our adventures in the multiverse, but how those adventures changed us, how they brought us closer to each other and to the universe."

The discussion went on for hours. They planned, they dreamed, and most importantly, they took the first steps toward making those dreams a reality. They contacted friends who worked in education and community organization, they sketched out a curriculum, and they set dates for their first public talks.

As the day turned into evening, Anika, and Sharvil felt a profound sense of purpose and joy. They were no longer just witnesses to the power of love; they were its ambassadors, ready to spread its message far and wide.

Their apartment, once just a place to live, had become a hub of cosmic planning. Each idea, each project, was a thread in the vast tapestry of the universe, woven by two people who had seen the power of love stretch across the multiverse and had brought it back to their small corner of the world.

Anika and Sharvil transformed their cozy living room into a makeshift studio, where they prepared to record their first series of talks about their experiences. As the camera started rolling, Sharvil adjusted his glasses, looking over at Anika with a reassuring smile, and began their session.

"Welcome, everyone," Sharvil started, his voice steady but filled with excitement. "Today, we're going to share something very special with you—a journey that has not only transformed our understanding of love, but also how we perceive our existence in this vast universe."

Anika, with her usual radiant enthusiasm, chimed in. "This journey took us beyond our own world, through the intricacies of the multiverse, where we discovered the profound connections of love that transcend time and space."

Sharvil nodded, picking up where Anika left off. "Our adventure began with what we thought was just a mythic manuscript, a poetic exploration of two ancient lovers, Aditya, and Lasya. But as we delved deeper, guided by the sage Kalanabha, we uncovered the real magic hidden within those texts."

Anika leaned forward, her eyes sparkling with the thrill of their tale. "These weren't just stories. They were reflections of universal truths, echoed through what we now understand as the Multiversal Mantras. These mantras weren't just spiritual; they had scientific dimensions, resonating closely with concepts like quantum entanglement."

"The idea that two particles, no matter how far apart, are connected in such a way that the state of one instantly affects the state of the other," Sharvil explained, making complex theories accessible. "This parallel isn't just a theory for us. We lived this connection, across dimensions, experiencing first hand the eternal bond shared by Aditya and Lasya—which, as it turned out, was our own bond in past lives."

Anika continued, "This realization wasn't just about past lives or esoteric truths. It brought us a message of unity and interconnectedness. It taught us that love, at its core, is a powerful force—a frequency that binds the universe."

Sharvil interjected, adding a practical aspect to their discussion. "And here's where it gets even more interesting. These experiences have influenced our daily lives. We practice mindfulness, gratitude, and intentionality, which stem from our deeper understanding of these cosmic connections."

"We want to share these insights with you to perhaps inspire a new way of looking at your relationships and the world around you," Anika said, her voice soft but persuasive. "Imagine living every day with the awareness that your actions are part of a larger cosmic dance—that your love, your kindness, your very existence, has ripples that extend far beyond what you can see."

Sharvil concluded their session with an invitation. "Join us as we explore these ideas further in our upcoming talks. We'll dive into how these ancient insights can be applied in modern contexts to help us live more connected and meaningful lives."

As the camera stopped recording, Anika and Sharvil relaxed back into their seats, exchanging a look of contentment and anticipation. They spent the rest of the day planning future topics, sketching out diagrams that blended scientific concepts with spiritual insights, and outlining their next talk, which would delve deeper into the practical applications of their discoveries.

That evening, as they reviewed the footage, they felt a profound sense of purpose. Their personal journey of discovery had grown into a mission to share their newfound wisdom, hoping to inspire others to see the universe and their place within it through a lens of love and interconnectedness.

Their lives had become a testament to the power of love, not just as a personal experience but as a universal truth, echoing the cosmic mantra that had guided them through the multiverse. As they prepared for the release of their first episode, they knew they were not just sharing a story—they were inviting the world to open its heart to the echoes of the cosmos.

In the soft glow of the evening light filtering through their home office window, Anika, and Sharvil sat across from each other, their laptop screens aglow with research papers and ancient texts. A large whiteboard stood to the side, filled with ideas and plans for their newly conceived foundation: Guardians of the Multiverse.

Sharvil, his eyes scanning through a detailed report on quantum physics, turned to Anika, his tone serious yet filled with excitement. "You know, Anika, starting this foundation could really bridge the gap between scientific inquiry and spiritual wisdom. It's about showing how interconnected these realms are, just like what we've experienced."

Anika nodded, her gaze fixed on a passage from an ancient Vedic text. "Absolutely, Sharvil. And think about how much we can offer by bringing these insights to a broader audience. It's not just about preserving these teachings but making them relevant for today's world."

Sharvil leaned back, pondering "Right. So, the main goal of our foundation should be to foster a deeper understanding of this integration. We could organize workshops, talks, maybe even collaborate with universities and research centers."

"Exactly," Anika responded enthusiastically. "And we should also focus on creating educational materials that can be used in schools. Imagine children learning early on about the interconnectedness of all things through both a scientific and spiritual lens."

Sharvil smiled, clearly inspired by the idea. "I love that. Education that doesn't just fill minds with facts but also teaches them to see the larger picture."

Anika, feeling a surge of inspiration, began typing rapidly. "Let's jot down some key initiatives, then. First, we'll need a solid programme for schools. Then, regular public seminars and perhaps an annual conference where we bring in experts from both fields."

Sharvil, now on his feet, paced thoughtfully. "We should also consider publishing a series of books or guides. Something that can serve as a reference for those who want to dive deeper into these concepts."

Anika nodded vigorously. "And not to forget, a digital platform—a hub where people from around the world can access our resources, learn, and even participate in discussions."

As they discussed, the room was filled with an air of creativity and purpose. Sharvil walked over to the whiteboard, adding each new idea under the appropriate heading. "This is going to be a huge undertaking, Anika. But it feels right, doesn't it?"

"It does," Anika agreed, her voice soft but firm. "It feels like a culmination of everything we've been through, everything we've learned. It's our chance to give back, to contribute something lasting to the world."

They decided to name their first initiative 'Quantum Vedic Fusion,' a programme aimed at exploring the scientific foundations of spiritual phenomena described in ancient texts.

As night deepened, they outlined a draft proposal for their first big event, planning to invite scholars, scientists, spiritual leaders, and the public to a symposium on science and spirituality.

The next morning, they reached out to contacts they had made during their travels and studies, pitching the concept of the foundation and inviting collaboration. The responses were overwhelmingly positive, fueling their enthusiasm further.

Weeks of preparation turned into months, and the foundation slowly took shape. They were meticulous in ensuring that each aspect of the foundation truly reflected the union of science and spirituality, from the design of their logo—a spiral galaxy enveloped by a lotus—to the content they curated.

Finally, the day came for the official launch of the Guardians of the Multiverse. Anika and Sharvil stood before a crowd gathered in a large auditorium, their hearts full of hope and excitement. They shared their story, their vision, and their belief in the transformative power of unified knowledge.

"Our journey through the multiverse taught us one incredible lesson," Anika addressed the audience, her voice clear and resonant. "That love and knowledge, science, and spirituality, are not separate. They are echoes of the same truth, seen through different lenses. Through this foundation, we invite you to explore these connections with us, to learn and grow together."

The applause that followed was not just in appreciation of their speech but a shared recognition of the journey ahead—a journey of exploration, understanding, and unity.

As they stepped down from the podium, Sharvil squeezed Anika's hand, a silent acknowledgment of how far they had come and the infinite possibilities that lay ahead. Together, they were ready to guide others through the cosmos, not just as travelers but as guardians of a profound multiversal wisdom.

In the quiet of their study, surrounded by books and artifacts collected from their extraordinary journeys, Anika, and Sharvil sat together, a serene silence enveloping them. It was an evening like many before, yet it held a palpable sense of culmination and introspection.

Anika, with a gentle smile, broke the silence. "It's incredible, isn't it? How far we've come, not just in miles, but in understanding and depth."

Sharvil nodded, his eyes reflecting a mix of nostalgia and wonder. "Yes, from stumbling upon that ancient manuscript to travelling through the multiverse. Every step seemed like a chapter from a grand epic written just for us."

Their journey had indeed been profound. Starting from the dusty shelves of a hidden library in Kerala to the ethereal realms of the multiverse, each adventure had deepened their bond and expanded their comprehension of the cosmos and its intricate dance of destiny and chance.

"Remember the first time we activated the cosmic portal?" Sharvil asked, a twinkle of mischief in his eyes.

Anika laughed, "How could I forget? I was terrified we'd end up on some alien planet. Instead, we got a front-row seat to the universe's greatest love story—ours."

That moment had been a turning point. Witnessing their past lives as Aditya and Lasya in a celestial ceremony had not only reaffirmed their love but had also revealed its timeless nature. It was a love not confined by temporal bounds, echoing across lifetimes and dimensions.

"It's more than just our story, though," Anika mused, her gaze distant but voice firm. "It's about the lessons we've learned about love's power, its resilience. How it transcends not just space, but time, adversity, even death."

Sharvil took her hand, feeling the familiar warmth that had always anchored him. "And now, we carry those lessons forward. Not just for us but for everyone willing to listen, to learn."

They had shared their experiences through talks, writings, and by founding the Guardians of the Multiverse, but their mission felt far from over. There were still realms to explore, mysteries to unravel, and countless ways to disseminate the wisdom they had garnered.

"As much as we've discovered, I feel like we're just scratching the surface," Sharvil said thoughtfully. "There's so much more out there—more connections to make, more echoes of our love to find in the cosmos."

Anika squeezed his hand in agreement, her spirit alight with the promise of continued exploration. "Let's keep going then. Let's keep seeking, sharing, loving. After all, every end is just a new beginning."

Their conversation drifted into plans for future travels, both literal and intellectual. They discussed revisiting some of the realms they'd encountered, diving deeper into the scientific and spiritual syntheses they had begun to understand.

As the night deepened, they stepped out onto their balcony, where the city lights twinkled below, mirroring the starry sky above. In this moment, between the vastness of space above and the grounding reality of Earth below, Anika and Sharvil felt a profound connection to everything.

The universe, with all its mysteries and magnificence, no longer felt like a distant, cold space. It was alive, resonant with the echoes of their love and the myriad connections they had forged.

With hands intertwined, they made a silent vow – to keep exploring, to keep loving, to keep living the legacy of wisdom and affection they had built. Their love, a testament to the enduring power of the human heart, promised to continue its journey across lifetimes and universes, leaving behind a trail of light for others to follow.

As they turned to go back inside, Anika paused and looked up at the sky, whispering, "Thank you, for the echoes, for the love, for everything." And the universe, in its timeless expanse, seemed to whisper back, acknowledging their small yet significant place in its grand tapestry.

Postscript: Embracing the Embroidery of Love

Dear Cosmic Traveller,

If you've journeyed with us through the pages of this book, by now you've walked alongside Anika and Sharvil, crossing realms, and living through the ebbs and flows of a love that redefined universes. You've been more than a passive observer; you've been a fellow traveller, an essential heartbeat in this grand adventure of love and legacy.

Isn't it fascinating? The power that stories have, the manner in which they can pull us in and make us feel things, perhaps even emotions we've never felt before? We traversed dimensions and challenged the very fabric of reality, but at its core, it was always about two souls finding, losing, and rediscovering each other. Love, as they say, is the most potent magic of all.

Each chapter, every whispered promise, every tear shed, was not just about Anika and Sharvil, but about us – about the power of human (and sometimes not-so-human) connection, about the universal longing to find someone who resonates with the melody of our souls. It's about that intangible 'something' that binds us, that makes distances seem trivial and time inconsequential.

At its heart, the tale you've just immersed yourself in speaks to a deeper truth we often overlook: that love is boundless. Its echoes aren't just heard in poetic verses or seen in grand romantic gestures but in the quiet moments. The understanding glances, the gentle squeeze of a hand, the silent promise to always be there, no matter which universe you're in.

Love is an eternal dance, one that takes on different forms but never truly ends. Like the most intricate of waltzes, it whirls, it dips, it soars, but always in harmony. Anika and Sharvil's journey was a dance, their souls intertwined in an ageless rhythm. Just as your own dance is unique, and every turn, every pause, is a step in the grand choreography of life.

And as this story concludes, remember that it's not truly an end. Stories like these, tales of such profound emotion, live on. They linger in the spaces between heartbeats, in the quiet sighs before dawn, in the soft glow of twilight. And if you ever find yourself gazing up at a starlit sky, remember that somewhere, in a universe not too far away, Anika and Sharvil are looking back, their love a radiant beacon for all to see.

In essence, this is a tale not just about love, but also about hope. The hope is that no matter the adversities, love will always find a way. Through time, through space, through the vastness of countless universes. Their journey, though special, is a mirror of ours. It's a testament to the power of commitment, faith, and the sheer resilience of the human spirit.

Now, as you close this book and return it to its place on your shelf, know that you're not just placing a collection of pages bound together, but a fragment of the multiverse, an echo of a timeless love story. And maybe, just maybe, it's inspired you to look at the world a little differently, to believe in the impossible, to love a little deeper, and to dance to the unique rhythm of your own universe.

As you step into tomorrow, let love be your guide. Embrace its highs, its lows, and all the moments in between. For in love, we find our truest selves.

With heartfelt gratitude and boundless love,
The Cosmic Embroidery Weavers